Jagged Shores

COLD DAY DAWNING

THOM COLLINS

Cold Day Dawning
ISBN # 978-1-80250-559-7
©Copyright Thom Collins 2023
Cover Art by Kelly Martin ©Copyright August 2023
Interior text design by Claire Siemaszkiewicz
Pride Publishing

COLD DAY
DAWNING

Dedication

For my husband Liam

Chapter One

Dalton Caine watched his sister as she moved around the party and wondered how many of these people were truly her friends. For as long as he had known her, Catherine had never been a social person, but now here she was, hosting a lavish bash for at least sixty guests and fluttering through the crowd like a society queen. Though she had waved to him from across the room, she had yet to speak to Dalton, who had arrived over half an hour before.

No surprise. Family had never featured high in her list of priorities.

Catherine had lost a lot of weight since he'd seen her last, so much that it worried him. Tonight, with her dark hair tied back in a severe ponytail, her features were drawn and sharp. It made her cheekbones appear more prominent and her wide mouth, painted a deep shade of red, seem huge. She wore narrow-legged trousers and a black jacket with nothing underneath, exposing the boniness of her chest. She talked animatedly with a group of men, gesturing throughout with a half-empty glass of white wine. While many of the guests held plates from the extravagant buffet, Catherine appeared to be avoiding the food.

He hadn't seen his sister in person for almost a year, and the signs were there that she was neglecting herself again.

Catherine put her free hand on the shoulder of one of her guests and threw back her head in a theatrical laugh. The sound carried across the terrace. Dalton noticed how most of the other attendees observed her with bemused interest, though none of them were laughing with her.

He knocked back the dregs of his vodka and tonic and headed to the bar for another.

Though it was mid-March and the evening had a spring chill about it, the party was taking place outdoors. Half the large terrace and garden had been covered by a temporary gazebo. Electric heaters and real fire pits were placed around to create a warm alfresco experience, despite the time of year. A pop-up bar was set on a raised patio to one side.

Dalton returned his empty glass and asked the bartender for another. It looked like it was to be a long and uneventful night. He might as well enjoy the free drinks, if nothing else. He had made several attempts to strike up conversation with Catherine's friends, but none could be roused for much more than a polite 'nice to meet you'.

As he waited for his drink, a middle-aged woman in a smart navy trouser suit sidled up next to him.

"Hi," he said.

She gave him a warm smile, tapping her ringed fingers on the piano-topped surface of the bar. "Hello."

"This is some party, isn't it?" he said, trying once more to start a conversation.

She frowned. "Oh, yes. Yes, it is. I know the caterers. They did my niece's wedding last summer. They are always very reliable."

"Are you a friend of Catherine's?" he asked, and when the woman frowned again, he elaborated, "I'm her brother...Dalton."

"Oh." She suddenly looked flustered. "It's lovely to meet you. Well, no, I don't know your sister well. My husband does business with Justin. That's the only reason we were invited, I think. You know how it goes — to grease the wheels and keep things turning."

Justin was Catherine's new boyfriend and owner of the McMansion where the party was taking place. Dalton had met him briefly upon his arrival. He seemed like a nice guy, a good few years older than Catherine. He appeared to have a down-to-earth attitude, despite his obvious wealth. *Grounded, even.* He was not at all what Dalton expected from one of Catherine's men. She tended to favour the young six-pack hunks who looked good on her social media posts.

"Do you live around here?" the woman asked, looking at him with renewed interest.

"No. I'm just here for the party and a chance to catch up with Catherine. I only arrived this afternoon."

"Oh, that's lovely. You must be staying here then...at the house."

He shook his head. "I've got a room at a hotel on the harbour. Quay House. It's beautiful."

"Hmm. We don't really know Nyemouth. We live in Morpeth. Nyemouth is...well, a bit too touristy for my taste." She lowered her voice. "And it's rough. You want to be careful down there. Don't go wandering around on your own…especially at night. I won't put a foot in the place, myself—not after all the things that have gone on." She gritted her teeth and grimaced.

Dalton flashed a good-natured smile. His drink arrived, and he excused himself. Like everyone else he'd tried to speak to, the woman seemed to be quite a snob. It was no surprise that Catherine surrounded herself with these types. She had always considered herself a cut above everyone else. Despite their comfortable middle-class upbringing, Catherine had never been satisfied with their status.

The house was indeed huge. Dalton had noticed as the taxi brought him here that it was the largest plot in an estate of modern mansions. It seemed natural that Catherine would have gravitated to the man who owned it. He had seen photos and videos of it on her Instagram account, but the images didn't do justice to the size of the place.

The other guests had separated into their small social bubbles, and no one seemed in the mood to mix with anyone from outside. Dalton couldn't take much more of this and sought out the reason for him being here.

Catherine was holding court with the same group of men. Dalton pushed straight in.

"Hey, sis," he said brightly.

She paused mid-sentence and a shadow of annoyance passed over her beautiful face, before she let out a loud shriek and threw her arms around him. "My little baby brother," she screamed.

Dalton winced. Catherine had looked thin from across the room, but it was only as he hugged her that he realised just how bony she had become.

"Guys," she said, spinning him around to face the group of men. "This is Dalton. Isn't he gorgeous? And single, if any of you fancy a ride."

Dalton shrivelled inside as four pairs of keen eyes looked him up and down. One of the men stepped closer, as though he believed Catherine had made a serious offer. Dalton gave a tiny head shake, and the man backed off. He didn't need his sister to pimp him out on top of everything else.

"This is so cool," Catherine cried. "C'mon, baby bro. We've got to get a picture for my socials." She flung the arm carrying the glass of wine around his shoulder and pulled him close, while thrusting her phone high above them. "Selfies, first."

Dalton gave a tight smile, keeping his teeth covered while Catherine took one photo after another for what seemed like minutes. Her breath was sour with wine, and he wondered just how much she'd had to drink, especially on an empty stomach.

"That should do," she said, tossing her phone to one of the hangers-on. "Now, video."

It was difficult to guess the age of the man who filmed them. His hair was highlighted, and his face was so puffy with fillers and Botox that he could have been anything from twenty-five to sixty.

Catherine leaned in even closer to Dalton. Her fingers went to his shirt and deftly undid two buttons.

"What are you doing?" he gasped, trying to stop her.

"You've got to make it sexy, darling." She opened his shirt and exposed his hairy chest. "My followers expect it."

"Now you're on," the man with the phone said. His lips curled back in an unpleasant, predatory smile...like a wolf.

Catherine pressed her face close to Dalton's.

"How do we look?" she asked.

"Perfect," the wolf replied.

Dalton fidgeted and tried to ease away, but Catherine's grip was unrelenting.

"Hey, guys," she addressed the camera in an even louder, falser voice than before. "I've got a real treat for you all. You're always messaging and telling me how much more you want to know about my life. Well, get a load of this...my cute little brother." She planted a sticky kiss on his cheek. "Isn't he gorgeous? I know you're all going to be fluttering over this post." *A loud, fake laugh.*

Dalton squirmed, somehow managing to maintain the fixed grin. This was all wrong. He hadn't seen his sister in so long, and she had turned their first serious catch-up into a social media post.

"Why don't you tell everyone where they can follow you?" Catherine pressed him, laying her head against his. "Everyone is going to want more of you."

"No kidding," one of her friends sniggered.

"Eh?" Dalton asked.

"Well, duh. Your Insta. Twitter. Where can people find you?"

"Oh," he said, feeling like a stunned mullet under the glare of the phone camera. "Well, they can't. I'm not on social media."

"Of course, you are. I know you are. Come on. Don't be shy."

Dalton's face, neck and ears burned red. He searched desperately for a solution. "My accounts are all private." He shrugged and gave an awkward glance to the camera. "Sorry."

"OMG. What's he like?" Catherine ruffled his hair. "Shy, as well as gorgeous. Well, don't worry, folks. I'll keep working on him. It'll only be a matter of time before he gets the bug and starts selling his nudes on OnlyFans." She gazed at the camera for another ten seconds before snapping her fingers. The wolf handed her back the phone.

Dalton stepped aside, grateful to have his personal space again.

"For fuck's sake." Catherine turned on him, waving the phone in his face. "You could at least have made some frigging effort. Do you know how many followers I have? How many people will see that? Oh my God, you're like a fucking zombie."

"Sorry. I'm not comfortable with all that stuff."

"*I'm not comfortable with all that stuff,*" she mimicked. Her posse of friends sniggered. "This is what I do. I'm a fucking *influencer*. I'm not even sure I can post this shit. My fans are going to think my brother is stupid."

"Then don't post it," he snapped. "I never asked to be in one of your posts."

"That's typical," she said, addressing herself to the acolytes. "It's par for the fucking course with my family. Most people would kill to be in one of my posts and associated with me, but not these fuckers. Ungrateful pricks."

Dalton took a deep breath. *Keep your cool.* "Sis, come on. I drove for almost seven hours to see you tonight. Don't be like this."

Catherine took a large swig of wine. "Like what? It's my party. I only want to share some of my happiness with my followers. You're the one who's too high and fucking mighty to pose for a selfie."

13

Stay calm. "We took a selfie, didn't we? It's the video I feel uncomfortable with. Come on. Why don't we go and have something to eat and a quiet catch up. The food looks delicious."

"Of course, it bloody does. I paid for it, remember? You go and stuff your face if you want to. I want to party and have a good time. C'mon, guys. Let's get more wine. Not the shit they're serving at the bar… I've got the good stuff hidden inside."

She spun on her heel and flounced off without a backward glance. The four men who had hung on her every word gave Dalton a final once over before following her trail.

Dalton shook his head and scratched the back of his neck. *She's drunk. Don't take it personally.* Catherine's and his relationship had always been up and down, but he had expected a slightly better welcome than that. As the only member of the family to make the journey from Surrey to Northumberland, he'd been hopeful it could be the start of something, the healing of a rift. *Wishful thinking.* Maybe things would be better tomorrow when she was sober. If *she was sober.*

He went in search of a bathroom. Open French windows led into a large dining room. It was no surprise to discover that the interior of the house was all style over substance—highly polished floors and white walls, with vague modern art in gilt frames. The dining table was a large white oval surrounded by twelve throne-like chairs covered in silver velvet. The whole impression was of something chosen by a designer, largely unused and uncomfortable.

He made his way into a hall with a grandiose staircase ascending to a mezzanine. The ceiling was one of the highest he'd seen outside of a hotel, with an enormous, crystal chandelier that could have come straight from a production of *Phantom of the Opera*. Only here, instead of the anonymous art of the dining room, were a series of framed black and white portraits of Catherine.

Dalton stopped to study them. The photos were nothing like the filtered selfies she posted online. They were all from the same session. Catherine was on a beach, wearing a plain white shirt, the wind tossing her shoulder-length black hair. The photographer had captured something quite lovely and natural about her. Her smile seemed easy, genuine, and in the more serious shots, when she gazed at the camera, there was a depth and character in her eyes that Dalton had not seen before. It was obvious, from the strength of the pictures, that Catherine could have been a successful model, like their mother, if she'd ever possessed the discipline and self-restraint to pursue the profession.

He gazed at each of the images for several minutes, absorbed by their beauty.

The spell was broken by the sound of a toilet flushing. A few moments later, a door on the right opened and a man stepped out. He caught Dalton's attention straight away. Dressed in jeans, a black T-shirt and a dark overshirt, the man looked nothing like the pretentious people he'd encountered so far this evening.

He was also very handsome, which didn't hurt. He was naturally good-looking, with brown hair, slightly wavy on the top and cut short at the back and sides where it was starting to turn grey. He had a serious-looking face, and Dalton's initial impression was of something quite sad about his eyes and downturned mouth.

"Hi," Dalton said cheerfully, hoping the guy wouldn't turn out to be like all the other guests.

"Hello." The man didn't return the smile, but seemingly noticing Dalton's interest in the photographs, he came closer. "Do you like them?"

There was a trace of an accent there. Dalton couldn't quite place it. Eastern European, he guessed.

"Very much," he replied. "They're remarkable. I've never seen Catherine like this before."

The man looked between Dalton and photographs. "I'm glad you like them. I took all of these."

Up close, he was even better looking than his first appearance. His eyes were dark grey and there was stubble on his square jaw, also flecked with grey.

"Wow," Dalton said. "They are sensational... really."

At last, his mouth turned upwards into the smallest suggestion of a smile. "Thank you." He held out his hand. "My name is Antoni."

Dalton accepted the handshake. The party had finally improved.

Chapter Two

Antoni Nowak had given up on love, sex and anything remotely romantic. He couldn't remember the last time he'd looked at a man and felt even a flicker of attraction. It seemed that part of his life was done with. But as he spoke to the stranger in the hall about his photographs, his skin tingled and his pulse quickened as he darted his gaze back and forth between the pictures and the stranger.

He was remarkably good-looking. Antoni's libido might have gone into early retirement, but his artistic eye for beauty had stayed strong. The man appeared to be in his early thirties and was an inch or two shorter than Antoni. He had a good physique — strong without being bulky. His face was symmetrical, with even, dark-brown eyes and a perfect, almost boyish smile. His dark hair was glossy and thick on top, short at the back and sides with long sideburns leading into a light beard.

The top three buttons of his blue shirt were undone, exposing the dark curls on his chest.

Antoni's breath caught as he looked at him, and the realisation dawned that this was the first guy he had fancied in months.

"My name's Dalton," the man said, shaking his hand. "It's nice to meet you."

"You, too." Antoni's mouth was dry, and his voice cracked. He ran his tongue around the inside of his gums, summoning saliva. Dalton looked at him intently. Antoni gestured to the photographs of Catherine as a distraction. "These were taken on the beach in town...down in Nyemouth."

Dalton looked back at the pictures. His profile was as strong and perfect as his face. "The light is incredible. Did you alter them or touch them up?"

"No, it's all natural. It was an early morning, last month. Very cold. You wouldn't think it, looking at the images, but Catherine had to suck ice cubes to reduce the breath caught on camera."

"You're kidding. She's only wearing a shirt."

Antoni chuckled. "Yes. My assistant was standing out of shot with a huge padded jacket and a hot water bottle. We could only shoot for a few minutes at a time before she needed to wrap up again. It's all illusion. It was freezing."

"Why not just take them in a studio? Or later in the year?"

"It was Catherine's idea to do the shoot on the beach. She was...er, quite insistent. I assumed she needed them for a deadline or a post she wanted to make. We did some others in colour to show off the shirt. I think maybe she got sponsored for wearing it. Something like that, anyway."

Dalton tutted lightly. "That makes more sense."

As well as his dreamy good looks, it was lovely to talk to Dalton. He was the only person at the party to show any interest in Antoni or the photos.

"So, are you based locally?" Dalton asked.

"Yes. I have a gallery in town with my brother."

"You do? Wow."

"The Nyemouth and Northumberland Gallery. I take pictures. Roger paints. We specialise in landscapes, coastal images, that kind of thing. But I've recently got into portrait photography."

"Why is that?" Dalton fixed him with those deep brown eyes. They were captivating.

Antoni looked away and shrugged. "Just to try new things, I guess. Broaden my horizons. These, I'm quite proud of. They turned out very well."

They looked at each other again and the silence grew uncomfortable. Antoni found small talk difficult at the best of times, so with the added complication of fancying Dalton, words seemed to desert him.

Dalton broke the spell. "I'm sticking around for a few days after the party. I want to explore Nyemouth a little. I'll drop by the gallery sometime."

Antoni froze. *Is he just being polite? Am I reading too much into this?* He was so out of practice with flirting of any kind, he had no clue. "That'll be cool. You can find us in the old town. We're on Pier Street. It runs behind the harbour."

Another flash of that boyish smile. "Brilliant. I haven't had time to look around yet, but I'll put that right tomorrow. I'll see you there?"

Antoni's face was warm, and he knew he must be blushing. "Definitely. I'll be there all day," he said, attempting to sound light. *Not too keen.*

"I'm looking forward to it already." Dalton gave his arm a gentle pat as he stepped aside and headed for the bathroom.

Antoni's head whirled. What had just happened? Had he misread the signs or was Dalton interested in him? *Surely not. No. I don't know left from right these days.*

One thing was certain. He didn't want Dalton to return from the bathroom and find him lurking there in the hall like a crazed stalker. How bad would that look? He hurried back to the party.

Most of the guests were still outside. He made eye contact and managed a smile as he walked by but found it impossible to start up a conversation with strangers. Most people were paired off or in groups, and it was an even more daunting prospect to speak to any of those. He picked his way to the bar for an orange and soda then found a bench in a secluded nook where he could hide in peace.

Social situations hadn't always been so painful. For years he'd played an active part in the local community and hosted fundraising events at the gallery. He'd sat on charity committees and had even taught a summer photography class for the Nyemouth youth club. He'd been outgoing and confident, with a wide circle of friends.

All that had changed one stormy night last October, when a madman with a knife had pursued a twisted course of revenge.

Antoni shuddered and pushed the thought away. This was not the place to dwell on that horror. He had sacrificed enough of his life to it.

He sipped his drink. It had gone nine o'clock. As soon as he finished this, he would go. Catherine would never know. She had barely noticed him all night.

When he had finished hanging her portraits that afternoon, she'd insisted he stay for her party. It would be good for him, she'd asserted. Her guests were very important people. They would be impressed by what he'd done, and it would surely lead to further commissions. She'd said she would have a grand unveiling of the pictures, but so far, that had failed to materialise. She hadn't said another word to him once her guests had arrived.

He wanted to go home. He was due to open the gallery in the morning and could do with a quiet night. There was no point to him going to bed early — insomnia had made a good seven hours of sleep a thing of the past — but he would rather be on his sofa catching up on *Master Chef* than wasting time at this party. He was several episodes behind, and it was just the kind of comfort TV he needed.

Catherine's false laugh cut across the terrace, rising above everyone else's conversation. Antoni groaned and tentatively raised his head to check on her position. He couldn't see her above the crowd, but it sounded like she was on the other side of the garden. As she'd barely noticed him all night, it would be a cruel twist if she caught sight of him just as he wanted to leave.

He pulled out his phone and checked for messages but found nothing of interest. His brother Roger was meeting his friends in the pub for a football match, so there was no chance of hearing from him. Harry and Christian, now his very best friends, were in the process of setting up a home together, so he didn't expect a peep from those two, either. All three of them had suffered at the hands of a maniac the past year. It was a miracle they had survived. Harry and Christian deserved the happiness they'd found together. Antoni didn't mind being alone, knowing his friends were doing all right.

It was now nine-fifteen. That was it…time to leave. He'd fulfilled his obligation to the hostess, even if she'd failed to return the favour. As long as she paid the invoice he would submit to her next week, that would be good enough. He left the empty glass on top of the bench where it would easily be found and, with his head bowed, crept across the terrace to the house. The quickest way out was straight through the dining room, to the hall and the front door.

Antoni was halfway across the room when Catherine and one of her friends, a flamboyant gay in his fifties, came through the other door. *Shit.* He could have sworn she was outside. They had their arms around each other's waist and their heads together as they laughed in a conspiratorial fashion. She paused mid-laugh and straightened when she saw him.

"Oh, Antoni, you're still here?" Catherine's eyes were glassy, and she rubbed her nose in the indiscreet way all cocaine users did when they'd taken a recent hit.

"I'm on my way out," he said, stepping aside to let them pass.

Catherine's male friend looked him over with predatory eyes before seeming to decide he was unworthy of attention. "I'll get us each another glass," he said, moving towards the door. "Same again?"

"No, babe. Get me a vodka cocktail, this time. I'll be right there." She turned her gaze to Antoni. The narrowing of her eyes made it obvious that she was wondering what he was doing there.

He shuffled from one foot to the other under the strength of her stare.

"So, you're happy with the portraits?" he asked.

She tossed her hair back over one shoulder, no longer smiling. "Of course. Why wouldn't I be? I look fucking hot in those snaps."

He stiffened. *Strange lady.* "I'm just checking. All part of the service. I'll leave you to your party."

She grabbed his elbow. "You'll get paid, if that's what you're worried about."

Antoni cringed and shook her loose. He did not appreciate the invasion of his personal space or the unwanted physical contact. "I'm glad to hear you like them, though I wasn't worried. I expect all my clients to pay their bills. I never thought you would be any different."

She snorted and tilted her head to look at him, a condescending smile on her face. For someone so naturally beautiful, it was an ugly expression. "You know, most photographers are grateful just to take my picture. They do it for free... For the publicity and all that."

"That wasn't our arrangement."

Undeterred, she said, "A good hashtag and a post on my account is worth more than any basic fee. Go on. Look me up. You'll see I'm one of the biggest influencers in the Northeast. Sure, the pro footballers have more followers, but I'm bigger than any of their wives and girlfriends, and my audience is growing all the time."

Antoni kept his cool. Roger had warned him something like this might happen. These minor celebrity types expected everything for free.

"That may be true in some cases, but unfortunately, in a small town like Nyemouth, hashtags don't keep the lights on or pay for expensive supplies and equipment.

As you're satisfied with my work, I'll submit my bill for our agreed amount. Good night and enjoy the rest of your evening." Antoni marvelled at his own composure. He treated Catherine to one last smile and a cordial nod before heading for the exit.

"You had better not have left any of your business cards lying around to clutter up the place," she called after him. "My guests don't want them, and they'll get chucked out with the rubbish in the morning."

He ignored her and kept walking. *What an intolerable woman.* It sounded like she intended to wriggle out of paying his fee after all. Well, she could think again. Other people might be prepared to accept her endorsement in lieu of actual payment, but not him. If she didn't settle within the required twenty-eight days, she would find herself in court with the prospect of having her all-important brand image tarnished. *The absolute cheek of it.*

He opened the front door and stepped outside, inhaling deeply. There were eight fancy cars parked on the drive, with many more lining the street beyond the boundary wall. His own vehicle, the gallery van, was parked at the edge of the estate. Although Catherine had insisted on him staying for her party, she'd also required him to move his van once her portraits had been installed.

"*It just won't do to have that on the driveway,*" she had told him.

He should have known then it was a bad idea to stay.

The night was chilly, and without the benefit of the patio heaters, he soon felt the cold. Antoni tucked in his chin and hurried through the gates.

"Hey, Antoni. Wait a minute, will you?"

He turned to see Dalton dashing towards him, pulling on a light jacket as he approached. Something inside Antoni flipped at the sight of him. *Gosh, he really is handsome.*

"Are you going back to town?" Dalton asked, drawing alongside, a perfect smile on his perfect face.

He nodded. "Yes."

"Any chance that you could give me a lift? I've already tried calling a taxi, but it's Friday night and there's at least an hour wait. There's no way I can stick out this party for another hour. I would walk, but it's my first night, and I don't really know where I am. I'm staying at Quay House, but you can drop me off anywhere that suits you."

Antoni found his easy-going manner completely disarming. Dalton was like no one else he'd met so far. "Yes, of course. I live above the gallery. I'll drive past your hotel on my way home. Come on. I'm parked a few minutes away."

They fell into matching steps beside each other.

"Pretty cold tonight," Dalton said, fastening his jacket.

Antoni nodded. "It's still early. We'll have cold mornings and evenings all the way through to May. Even then, it won't warm up properly until June, at least. We're pretty far north here."

"I'm learning that." From the corner of his eye, he saw Dalton turn to look at him. "So, er…I heard a bit of that conversation you had with Catherine. I thought if you were leaving, I would hitch a ride with you. I hope you don't mind."

He chuckled softly. "Not at all. I was leaving anyway, before that…er, altercation."

"Do you really think she'll try to scam you on the fees for those pictures?"

"We'll see. I hope not. I put a lot of time and effort into them. And the frames alone are worth several hundred pounds each."

"Shit. And she expects them for nothing?"

"Well, she didn't really say that."

"It's what she insinuated."

"Hopefully she'll come to her senses in a few days," Antoni said. They reached the white van with the Nyemouth and Northumberland Gallery logo stencilled on the side panels. "This is it," he said, pulling out his keys. He climbed into the driver's seat and turned on the engine.

After he got in, Dalton blew into his hands and rubbed them together.

Antoni turned the heating up to full. "It will warm up soon."

Dalton laughed. "I'm not used to this kind of cold."

He had a lovely voice—deep, but soft and full of humour and warmth.

"The bar at Quay House has a couple of real log fires. They should be lit tonight. Once you're settled in front of them, you'll soon warm up."

Antoni put the van in gear and pulled out into the road. He couldn't wait to get back to the real Nyemouth. This fancy estate with its modern mansions and shallow residents was not part of the town he knew and loved.

As he returned to the marina, with a charming companion along for the ride, the night was ending on a better note than it had begun.

Chapter Three

The traffic into the town centre was light, and Antoni pulled up in front of Quay House five minutes after leaving Catherine's. Nyemouth was quiet for a Friday night. It was early in the year, and although the tourists would start to return around Easter, the holiday season wouldn't really begin until May.

From his peripheral vison, he saw Dalton turn in his seat to look at him. Antoni squirmed, uncomfortable under the direct gaze of his dark eyes. "Have you got time to come in?" Dalton asked. "I'd like to buy you a drink…to thank you for the lift."

"Oh." Antoni gripped the wheel as his pulse quickened. His first reaction was to refuse. He'd had more than enough social contact for one day. He wanted to go home, lock the door and spend some quiet time alone, but Dalton was making him react in strange, unaccustomed ways. It wasn't just how good he looked. Antoni suspected the personality behind the gorgeous face was just as sweet. And the unfamiliar scent of him, the freshness of his body and hair combined with the sexy citrus notes of his aftershave, had a potent effect. "Erm, okay. Why not? A drink. Yes."

Dalton's teeth glinted in the dull light. "Great. Thanks."

"Let me get rid of the van," Antoni said, thinking practically. "The gallery is just over the river. I can park and be back here in ten minutes. Okay?"

"Perfect. I'll get the drinks. What's it to be?"

"Oh, just a beer. Thanks."

"Any particular brand? Bottle?"

"A pint of draught will be fine. Whatever they're serving."

Dalton unbuckled his seat belt. "I'll get them and find a table. See you in a few minutes." He swung his legs out of the van and flashed another of his sexy smiles before closing the door and hurrying up the steps to the front entrance of the hotel.

Antoni laughed out loud and pulled back onto the road. This was crazy. Dalton was definitely flirting with him. He was sure of it and couldn't work out a reason. Did he need glasses? Dalton was so smart, with his expensive-looking shirt and jacket and his lovely thick hair. *What does he see in me?* Antoni made so little effort with his appearance these days. As long as his clothes were clean and his hair was cut short enough to stay tidy, he was very low maintenance.

He hadn't always been this basic. He used to make the effort when he was with Harry. And even before then, he'd always liked to look good. Since last October, his physical appearance had been at the bottom of his priority list.

He felt shabby beside a man like Dalton, who was sharp enough to be a model.

Still, he had committed to the drink and had to honour it. If nothing else, visiting the bar would be another step on his path to recovery. Besides meals with family and friends and a couple of lunches at the Seagull Café, he had barely been out in months.

He crossed the bridge to the south bank and headed up the narrow, cobbled road of Pier Street. During the day, it was a nightmare trying to get the van along this way. The route was always packed with pedestrians, but at this time of night, he had a clear run all the way to the gallery. He pulled up to the rear and parked in the tiny yard that doubled as a garage. Locking the gate, he hurried back the way he had come. His nerves jangled and his pulse was quick. He sucked in deep, open-mouthed breaths, following the techniques he had been taught to get his anxiety under control.

It's just a drink... One beer with a friendly stranger. There's nothing to worry about.

He entered Quay House by the ground floor entrance, which led straight into the bar. It was busy but not full. He stuck to the edges of the room, avoiding the more crowded areas in the centre as he looked for Dalton among the mass of unfamiliar faces.

A hand waved at him from the other side, and he caught sight of that lovely face again.

Wow, he really is gorgeous.

Flushed, certain his embarrassment and awkwardness must be written all over his face, he made his way across the room. Dalton had secured one of the high-backed leather booths, and Antoni slid in opposite him, where a full pint waited on the table. Dalton had a glass of white wine.

"That was quick," Dalton said. "It didn't seem like ten minutes at all. It took me all that time to get served."

Antoni sipped the beer and licked the foam from his top lip. "I'm a fast walker. People always tell me to slow down."

"It must be those long legs of yours," Dalton said. "It's not easy for tall people to walk slowly."

Heat stung his cheeks again, and he took another swallow. "That must be it."

Dalton had taken off his jacket and rolled up the sleeves of his blue shirt. Antoni gazed at the fine dark hair that coated his forearms. It was easier and less disarming than looking at his face.

Dalton sat straight, with both of his hands on the table. "I've got something to confess."

"Oh." *Here it comes. I've read this all wrong. Damn. Of course, he doesn't fancy me at all.*

"I've been wondering the whole time you've been away whether to say anything or not. It's not that big a deal, but you'll probably think it's strange that I didn't mention it earlier." He gave a shy, embarrassed laugh and took a sip of wine before looking at Antoni again. "So...the thing is...Catherine is my sister."

"Oh." *Not what I expected.* "She is?"

"Yeah." Dalton leaned back in his chair and seemed relieved of his burden. "I know, it seems a strange thing to make a big deal about. Why didn't I say something before? Well, after I heard the way she spoke to you, I was embarrassed. I didn't want you to think that I...well, that I'm like her, because I'm not."

Antoni laughed, and some of his tension eased. "It's kind of obvious...that you're not like her, I mean." Apart from their dark hair, there appeared to be no real family resemblance. Catherine's features were sharp, with a hard edge. She had a narrow nose and thin lips, where Dalton's face was fuller and warmer. Their eyes were different, too. Dalton's were deep and chocolatey, where Catherine had the eyes of a tiger, with shades of green, amber and gold.

"Yes, I'm more like my brother. The two of us are very alike and take after my dad's side of the family. Catherine is the eldest and more like our mum in looks."

"How old are you?" Antoni asked. He was curious and guessed late twenties, early thirties, but this seemed like an appropriate time to ask.

"Thirty-one. Catherine is thirty-seven. Tobias is in the middle, he's thirty-four, but I've always been closer to him. I guess because we're boys and nearer in age. When we were growing up, Catherine seemed so much older than us — more like another adult than a kid."

"I hope I didn't say anything to offend you earlier," Antoni said. "About your sister. If I'd known you were related…"

Dalton raised his hands. "Hey, it's fine with me. I'd have said a lot worse if I were in your position. We might be related but she's… Well, to be honest, she can be a real bitch. She always has been. And don't take it personally — her trying to screw you on your deal — she does that with everybody."

Antoni was shocked. "I've never heard anyone talk about a family member like that."

Dalton shrugged. "We're not like the average family." He laughed. "You know, I'm the only one who came for the party. I'm sure I was the only one she invited, but if she had asked the others — my brother, my parents — they wouldn't have come anyway. I'm the only one who is on any kind of speaking terms with her right now. And as you can probably guess, even I don't have the warmest relationship with her."

"I'm sorry."

"Oh, no need for that. It's the way it's always been between us. There were years when I didn't get on with her, either. Catherine was always rather complicated. She's had issues for as long as I can remember. It was only when I grew up that I started to understand some of them. When I went to university, I had friends who also needed help, and they opened me up to some of Catherine's problems. I decided it was time to get over myself and the prejudices my parents had given me against her. I was about twenty-three when I first reached out to her. We're still not close, not in any manner, but we try." He looked at his hands on the table, as though lost in thought, apparently reliving some traumatic family history, then looked at Antoni again. "You probably know her as well as I do. Your portraits are fantastic. How did that come about? What was she like to work with?"

"Oh," Antoni said, sitting back, wondering what he should reveal. Dalton seemed willing to be honest about his sibling's faults, but Antoni was a professional and Catherine was one of his customers. She might not have paid him for his services yet, but he had a responsibility to her.

"It's okay. You don't have to hold back on my account."

"It's not that. I shouldn't gossip about my clients."

"Oh, sure. Sorry… I shouldn't have asked."

"It's all right. I'll say it wasn't the easiest of days, but that might not have been entirely Catherine's fault. The work she wanted—you know, social media content? That's not my specialty. Like I said earlier, I tend not to photograph people at all, and specialise in landscapes. But when she approached me with the idea, I thought it would be a challenge, something to get me out of my comfort zone. And we did the shoot down on North

Beach, so I was still working in my natural environment, to some degree."

"Your photos are wonderful, full of atmosphere and character."

"I'm not sure that's what Catherine had in mind, but she seemed to like the results in the end—enough to have me frame a selection for her home. I'm pleased with how they turned out, too. I'm not sure I'll be in a hurry to work with a social media influencer again, but it was an experience, all right."

They both laughed.

"You know, I'm not convinced by how much of an influencer she really is," Dalton said. "I don't know much about that stuff, but Catherine has a few hundred thousand followers. That's a lot, sure, but don't the really big influencers have, like, millions? I don't think she's as big as she likes to make out." He shrugged. "Who cares, right? As long as it makes her happy."

"There's also her bar," Antoni said. "She has a cocktail bar on the other side of the river. It's just a five-minute walk from the gallery. A lot of her social media content is designed to promote that."

"Oh, yeah. I'd forgotten it. What's it like?"

"If you're in Nyemouth for a few days, you should check it out yourself."

Another flash of Dalton's boyish smile. "I see what you did there. You're not going to bad mouth your client's business, either."

"I'm the wrong person to ask about cocktail bars. This is the first time I've been out in the evening in a long time. Like I said, it's not very far. You should try it." This was not the time to mention Ethan, his young assistant at the gallery. Ethan used to work at Catherine's bar, White Lady, and quit because of the intolerable behaviour of his boss. The young man didn't have a good word to say about her.

Dalton put his elbows on the table and leaned closer. "How about we try it together? Tomorrow night? Saturday. Sounds like the perfect time for cocktails."

Antoni stiffened in surprise. There could be no more doubt about it. Dalton *was* flirting with him. "I thought you said you wanted to visit the gallery."

He wiggled his eyebrows. "I do. I'm a stranger in town for a few days. I've got to get to know the place. Art, cocktails — sounds like a good way to start."

Antoni's smile wavered as he considered his options. This was very sudden and unexpected. He wasn't looking for romance or even sex. They hadn't mattered to him in a long time. Could there be any harm in a brief flirtation? Dalton had admitted he was only here for a few days. If Antoni didn't get too involved, it could even be fun. "What is it you do?" he asked, changing the subject. He wasn't confident or comfortable enough to pursue the playful game Dalton had started.

"I run a property development company in Surrey. It's not as grand as it sounds. It's really just me and my business partner, Allegra. We buy neglected properties, bring in a team of contractors to restore and modernise them, then sell them on, hopefully for a nice profit. But we work well together, and I enjoy it. I can even turn my hand to some of the easier renovation jobs. I'm pretty handy with a sledgehammer and knocking down walls."

"You're wrong. That does sound impressive."

He shrugged. "I find being an artist or a photographer more impressive. I do enjoy the creative aspects of the business, though. Once the bricks-and-mortar stuff is out of the way, I enjoy the decorating side the most, choosing paint, tiles, flooring and all that. It's not the same as what you do, but it lets me be creative in my own small way."

Dalton drained the last of his wine. Antoni didn't have much beer left and emptied his glass. "Another?" he asked, feeling emboldened.

"I'll get them," Dalton said, shuffling across his seat. "I owe you for the lift."

Antoni waved his hand and stood. "No. You already did that. It's my turn. What is that you're drinking?"

"Chardonnay," Dalton answered. He reached across the table and rested his hand lightly on top of Antoni's. "I'll let you get these on one condition. When you return from the bar, you'll give me an answer about tomorrow night. Cocktails at Catherine's bar. *Please.*"

Antoni gave a soft shake of his head. He had never met anyone quite like this—someone so confident in asking for what he wanted. "Okay. I'll think about it."

He couldn't stop himself from smiling while he waited his turn at the bar, despite being totally conflicted. What would he do tomorrow, anyway? Spend another night alone in the flat, binge-watching cookery and TV talent shows? Hiding from the world again? Dalton was forward, probably too sure of himself for Antoni's liking, but he seemed like a nice guy. Unlike his sister, there appeared to be no dangerous edges to him.

A date with Dalton, if a date was what he was offering, would do him some good.

Dalton was waiting, a cheeky, expectant grin on his face, when Antoni returned to the booth with fresh drinks. "Well?" he enquired.

Antoni nodded. "All right. You're on. I'll see you in the gallery at some point tomorrow, and if you still want to afterwards, I'll go to the bar with you."

Dalton licked his lips. "Oh, there's no doubt about that. I definitely want to see more of you, Antoni."

Chapter Four

Dalton woke the next day to a pale blue sky showing at the window. He had a harbour-view room on the third floor of Quay House and had fallen asleep with the curtains open. The view was nice enough, but he was already thinking about Antoni. He flung back the covers and stepped out of bed with a smile, eager to see the guy again. He couldn't remember when he'd last met a man who'd been on his mind the second he opened his eyes.

Antoni was someone special. Dalton had realised that already, but he was deep, too. There had been none of the usual flirty small talk last night. Antoni had been serious all the way. So serious, in fact, that Dalton had doubted whether he would accept his invitation for a drink when they got back to town. It had taken all his charm and persuasion to convince him. It wasn't like Antoni wasn't interested in him, either. Dalton knew when a guy was keen.

Antoni didn't make it obvious. He didn't appear the type to crumble when someone paid him attention or to drop his trousers for a smile. That was what made him adorable.

Dalton had had his fill of superficial gays who were only interested in where their next shag was coming from. When his last relationship had ended, he'd downloaded a couple of dating apps and checked out the local scene for a few weeks. What a mistake that had been. The men he'd met were interested in one thing, and they made no secret of it. He had gone on three dates with a guy called Krish. Krish had seemed different to the rest—interested in more than a quick fuck. Dalton had thought there was something between them, until Krish had ghosted him right before Christmas. He'd later suspected that Krish was married and using the apps to secure some no-strings sex.

Though Antoni had shown signs of being into him the previous night, he obviously had no interest in jumping into bed with someone he'd just met.

Which only made him more attractive.

Dalton wasn't blind. Antoni was fantastically good-looking, but that wasn't everything. The chance to connect with a man who had more than one thing on his mind was too good an opportunity to waste. So what if Dalton was only here for a few days. They could still get to know each other.

He couldn't wait to look around the gallery and connect with Antoni again.

Before turning in, he'd put the Nyemouth and Northumberland Gallery into a search engine and spent a good while in bed, browsing through some of his photography. Antoni hadn't been exaggerating when he had said he specialised in landscapes and natural settings. Dalton couldn't find a single photo that was anything like the portraits he'd taken of

Catherine. He wasn't familiar with this area, but if Antoni's work was anything to go by, there were some fantastic sights and beautiful scenery to be found all along the coast—beaches, coves and bays, moorland, woods and waterfalls. Antoni's moody style captured the dramatic splendour in a way that made Dalton want to discover more.

He relieved himself in the bathroom and took a hot, invigorating shower. He wanted to look his best today, so he washed his hair, thinking about Antoni while he lathered up. He couldn't get those deep grey eyes out of his mind. They were beautiful and yet seemed filled with an unspoken sadness.

Antoni was a man with secrets. Dalton wondered if he would be lucky enough to discover them.

When he'd finished in the shower, he dried off and opened the suitcase he'd had no time to unpack when he'd arrived. He was booked here until Monday. Dalton laid out the clothes he needed for the day and packed the rest away in the wardrobe. He wanted to go for a casual but smart look and opted for black jeans, a white crew-neck T-shirt and a black jacket. The weather looked great so far, but he could always call back later if he needed something warmer.

This was good for now.

Ten minutes later he was in the hotel restaurant. It was located on the first floor and directly above the bar. The place was less than a quarter full, and he found a table by the window, looking out onto the River Nye and the old town on the other side. There hadn't been time to take it in when he'd arrived. He'd left his car in the public carpark down the road, checked into the hotel and got a taxi straight to Catherine's place.

The town was truly grand, with its wide harbour and the mixture of modern and old buildings lining the banks. Several people at the party had made snotty remarks about Nyemouth, but from where he sat now, it looked good to him.

A young woman in a hotel uniform came across to offer the menu and take his drinks order. He asked for apple juice and English breakfast tea, and when she returned with those, he ordered a full vegetarian breakfast. He hadn't realised until he'd come in and smelled the food how hungry he was. Despite the lavish buffet the past night, he hadn't eaten much. He had warned Catherine in advance that he was a vegetarian, but she hadn't passed the information on to her caterer. There had been little apart from salad he'd been able to eat.

Dalton settled back to admire the view. Antoni's gallery was somewhere on the other side of the river. If the map he had found was correct, it was tucked away down one of the back streets. It couldn't be far, he reasoned, given how quickly Antoni had parked his van and met him at the bar afterwards.

It was coming up to nine o'clock and they didn't open until ten, so there was no rush. He didn't want to get there straight away. Though he was keen, it wouldn't be cool to look that eager.

He jolted at the surprise vibration of his phone in his jeans pocket. Dalton pulled it out and glanced at the screen. *Unknown caller*. He thought about rejecting it, but as his finger was about to hit the button, he changed his mind and answered.

"Hello."

There was a pause before an unfamiliar voice said, "Oh, hi. Is this Dalton?"

The caller hadn't asked for Mr. Caine, which made them unlikely to be a spammer. "It is, yes. Who's calling please?"

He heard a release of breath on the other end. "Oh, hi. Sorry, yes. My name is Justin. I'm Catherine's boyfriend. I saw you across the room last night, but we were never introduced. Catherine tried to do the honours later, but you had left by then."

Dalton was aware his sister had a boyfriend. They'd been seeing each other for a few months. At least, according to her Instagram they had. She had posted a handful of photos of her with a man around fifty years old. He had receded grey hair and a nice smile. Dalton was sure the McMansion belonged to Justin, especially as she'd tagged some of his photos none-too-subtly with #sugardaddy.

"Hi, Justin. Sorry I didn't stick around. I was tired and had the chance of a lift back to the hotel. It seemed like a great party, though."

"Oh, well, sure. Don't worry about it. There'll be other parties."

Dalton laughed, a little nervously. Where was this heading? He hoped Justin wasn't about to rope him into some extravagant surprise for his sister—especially not today, when he was looking forward to seeing Antoni. "I hope so. I'm sure I'll get to see you before I leave, too. Maybe tomorrow?"

"Yes, yes, that sounds great."

Dalton frowned. Justin sounded nervous. Or was he misjudging this?

"Er...listen," Justin continued. "Catherine isn't with you, is she?"

"What? You mean right now? No, I'm at my hotel, just about to have breakfast. I thought she would be with you."

"Oh." Now he sounded disappointed. "No, she was gone when I got up this morning. I had a lot to drink last night so I didn't notice she wasn't here until I woke up about half an hour ago."

"Is that so strange?" Dalton asked. "Catherine still has her own place, doesn't she?" He couldn't remember her ever telling him that she'd moved in with Justin permanently.

"She still has the flat, yes. It's just that...well, all her stuff is here. She brought a small case because she was going to spend the weekend with me. It's still here — her clothes, all her makeup, her jewellery. I've tried calling her, but there's no answer."

Dalton wondered how well Justin knew his sister and how much he should reveal about her. "Maybe she's gone for a walk," he suggested. "Or a run. If she had a hangover herself, she might have gone for some fresh air to clear her head. I assume the party ended late."

"Yeah...maybe." Justin didn't sound convinced.

"I take it this isn't usual," he asked tentatively. "For her to go off without telling you?"

"Well, we don't keep twenty-four-hour tabs on each other. Nothing like that, but she was supposed to spend the weekend with me, and she's not here."

"The two of you didn't have a fight, did you? An argument at the end of the evening?"

"No. Of course no. Not one wrong word."

"I wouldn't worry too much. She's probably gone for that walk — or maybe to the shops. She might even have gone to pick up breakfast to surprise you," he said, trying to sound optimistic. "You've only been up half an hour."

"It's so unlike her," Justin said, "to not even answer her phone. What if she's been gone all night?"

Do you have any wealthy friends? Richer than you are?

Dalton immediately reproached himself. He shouldn't be bitchy. He knew his sister well enough not to worry over something like this, but it was obvious Justin was concerned.

"Listen," he said, choosing his words with care. "I don't know how long you guys have been together, and Catherine will probably kill me when she hears I've told you this, but it's nothing. I promise." When Justin didn't respond, he continued. "So, for as far back as I can remember, like, to when I was a little kid, Catherine used to do things like this — mainly to drive our mother crazy. Whenever the two of them argued over something, usually the most trivial thing, Catherine would pull a disappearing act. She would go missing for hours. She once ran away for a few days. Our parents were climbing the walls, the police were out looking for her and there was even a report on the TV."

Justin gasped.

"You see," Dalton said hurriedly. He didn't want to panic him. "I knew I shouldn't have said anything. And that's probably not what has happened now. But that's just the way Catherine is. When things get a bit too intense for her, she takes herself away for a little while. Are you sure you didn't have words last night?"

"No... Well, I don't think so. I was drunk."

"Then that's probably it. Catherine will be upset about something you don't even remember. She'll ignore your calls for a couple of hours, just to let you know that she's pissed off, and you'll hear from her this afternoon."

He'd already said too much. Catherine would lose her shit when she found out he had spoiled the perfect version she would want to project to Justin. The poor guy obviously had no idea of the kind of woman he was involved with. They couldn't have been together long, he reasoned, because she couldn't maintain her nice façade for any length of time. Sooner rather than later, her temper would boil to the surface.

"You seem very sure of this," Justin said. "So, you're not worried about her?"

Dalton wondered what kind of man Justin was, to freak out because his girlfriend had been absent for less than an hour. Was he the overbearing, needy type who had to know what his partner was doing every minute of the day? If that were the case, Justin and Catherine were a match made in hell, because she hated to be controlled or told what to do...*ever*.

He remembered the creepy gay guys she'd been with the previous night. They had seemed pretty tight. "I'm probably way off the mark with what I've suggested so far. She could have gone to breakfast with some of her mates. You know what her Instagram is like. She's always posting pictures of her brunches. She's probably out there making new content. You shouldn't worry. She's a grown woman."

Justin sighed. "I know. But she's so precious to me — and she needs me. I worry about her all the time."

Okay, these two really are a poor match. Catherine has found a man she can wrap around her finger and tie in knots. A terrible combination.

"Try not to. It's early. Have some breakfast if you haven't already and try to relax. Call me later if you haven't heard from her."

Dalton hung up and exhaled. *Oh boy.* What the hell was his sister up to now? She had a knack for pressing people's buttons and getting them stressed out—a skill she had mastered and honed with their parents from a young age. For Justin, someone he had never met before, to call him out of the blue on a Saturday morning and ask where she was showed she had someone else under her spell.

He was about to try her number himself when his breakfast arrived. Dalton put his phone down. Whatever manipulative game his sister was playing, it could wait. She'd already got Justin's day off to a bad start. Dalton was determined not to get caught up in whatever drama she had created this time.

Chapter Five

"There's someone here to see you," Roger Nowak said as he entered the stockroom.

Antoni was in the middle of packaging a customer order for one of his signed and numbered lithographs. He looked up, caught the knowing glint in his brother's eyes and knew what it meant. His stomach flipped. Dalton was here.

"Oh." He tried to sound casual and continued sealing the cardboard packing case.

Roger came up to the edge of the table. He folded his arms and fixed Antoni with a stare, a smile twitching at one side of his mouth. "He said you were expecting him."

Antoni couldn't resist a smile of his own, though his fingers trembled as he tried to secure the tape on the parcel. "That's right."

"Do I have to drag the details out of you?" Roger said with good-humoured exasperation. "Come on... Who is he?"

Antoni shrugged. "To be honest, I barely know him. We only met last night at Catherine Caine's party. He's her brother."

Roger's face stiffened. "Oh."

"It's okay. He's nothing like her."

"I should hope not." He grimaced. Roger was no fan of Nyemouth's resident influencer. "One is more than enough."

"We had a drink at Quay House after the party."

His brother brightened again. "Antoni, that's great."

Roger had always been protective of him, but never more than in the last six months. He had recently moved out of Roger's house, where he'd spent most of his recovery time, and back into his own flat above the gallery. Roger worried about him being on his own so much and had done his best to encourage Antoni to get out more, inviting him to the pub and for meals, which he rarely accepted. Being out in public, where most of the locals knew what had happened to him, was too uncomfortable. Antoni hated the unwanted attention. He'd promised Roger that later, when Nyemouth was busy with tourists and there were more people who didn't know him, he would socialise more.

Having gone to Quay House last night with Dalton was a huge deal. They both knew it.

"So, who is he? This guy from the party?" Roger pressed.

"His name is Dalton. He's Catherine's brother, like I told you. He lives in Surrey and he's only here for a few days, so don't put any expectations on this, okay?"

"Hey. He got you out for the night. That's a good enough start for me. And he must be keen, if he's come to see you already."

"We arranged it last night. He wanted to see the gallery."

"I bet he does. And that's not all." Roger looked even happier. "Oh my God. I'm so pleased for you, brother. Come on. What are you waiting for? Stop messing about back here. Get in there and see him."

"I'll just finish this," he said, returning to the packing job.

"The hell you will." Roger grabbed him by the elbow and pulled him aside. "There's a hunky man waiting for you, and he's already put the best smile on your face that I've seen in months. Go. *I'll* finish this."

"All right, I'm going." Antoni laughed.

He tried to play it cool for the benefit of his brother, but his insides were in a turmoil of nervous excitement. He wouldn't tell Roger, but Antoni had spent more time thinking about Dalton than he'd expected. He hadn't been this into a man since his last serious boyfriend, Harry Renner. It was crazy when they barely knew each other. They had spent two hours together, at most. Antoni was a realist. He followed his head, not his heart, and his head told him this was unworkable. There was no denying his instant attraction to Dalton, but it was nothing more. Whatever else he thought he was feeling, he had to ignore it. Dalton was a nice man in town for a few days and looking for local company. It was nothing more serious than that. It couldn't be.

Except Antoni had thought about little else all morning. Trying to stay busy with mundane tasks around the gallery, he hadn't been able to keep his eyes off the clock for long or himself from wondering when Dalton might arrive.

They hadn't arranged a time.

He checked his appearance in the bathroom mirror before going out front. He wore the usual smart-casual attire he always did for work — grey chinos and a white polo shirt. He had trimmed his stubble that morning and calmed some of the natural waves in his hair. Antoni rarely spent much time on his appearance, and this was as good as it got. With a deep breath, he headed through the public viewing area.

Dalton was in the room that contained the bulk of Antoni's black-and-white landscape photographs. Apart from a middle-aged couple farther along, he was alone. He must have heard Antoni approach and turned to greet him as he entered.

Antoni's insides did another gargantuan flip.

It was as if he had forgotten how handsome Dalton was overnight and was floored by the freshness of his beauty. His pulse accelerated from normal to racing in a second.

"Good morning." Dalton grinned and came towards him, arms wide, inviting a hug.

Antoni stiffened and raised a hand in defence. Dalton caught the cue and backed off at the last minute. As attractive as he was, Antoni was far from ready for any physical contact from a stranger. Even Roger and the rest of their family knew better than to crowd his personal space.

"Morning," he said, nervously trying to deflect from the awkwardness of his rejection. "Sorry… I'm not a touchy-feely person." *True.* Even before the attack, Antoni hadn't been the biggest fan of public displays of affection, only it had gotten a lot worse since.

Dalton raised both hands. "My fault. Me and my friends are very over-familiar with each other. I must remind myself that not everyone is comfortable with uninvited hugs."

Antoni nodded, gazing at the floor before forcing his attention back to Dalton. "It's good to see you again."

"And you, too. You have no idea how much."

Antoni drew a quick breath and blushed. Compliments had always been trouble for him, too.

Dalton deflected and turned his interest back to the photographs. "These are wonderful. I thought the pictures you took of Catherine were great, but these are something else."

"Thanks," he said, relaxing a little. It was easier to talk about his work than himself.

"These landscapes... Are they all of Nyemouth?"

"Pretty much... Within a few miles of here, anyway. The one you're looking at was taken from the South Pier, looking up at the cliffs late one evening as the sun was going down."

"Stunning."

He took Dalton on an impromptu tour of the room, explaining the locations in all the images.

"I have to get one of these to take home," Dalton said. "It's exactly what I need for my dining room. Though narrowing it down to one is going to be hard. I love all of them."

"Let me know when you decide, and it's all yours, no charge."

Dalton's good-natured expression turned serious. "Hey, I'm not my sister. I'll pay the full ticket price for anything I choose. I don't expect any favours."

"Sorry. I didn't mean to offend you."

The boyish smile returned. "You haven't. I don't like to take advantage, that's all. Of *anyone*." He shrugged. "I might have to come back later, though. There's too much good stuff to choose from for me to make an instant decision."

Antoni sensed they were being watched and when he turned to the counter, he saw Roger and their part-time assistant, Ethan, paying close attention.

"How is it going?" Roger hollered cheerfully.

"Fine," he shot back, pulling a face that told Roger to back off.

Roger and Ethan pretended to busy themselves with something on the laptop, looking very smug and pleased with themselves.

Antoni turned back to Dalton. "Would you like to go for a coffee? It will give you time to think about which of these you like."

Dalton's dark eyes danced across Antoni's face. "Good idea. You know this town better than I do, so lead the way."

"Let me grab a jacket."

Antoni collected his wallet and coat from the stockroom. "I'm going out for a little while," he told Roger, when he returned to the counter.

"Take all the time you want," his brother said. Then, lowering his voice, "I'm serious. He seems nice. Take the rest of the day off if you want to."

"I'll be back," Antoni told him, secretly pleased that Dalton had secured his brother's approval.

The sun had yet to reach the narrow cobbles of Pier Street, and there was a sharp chill in the air when they stepped out, turning their breath to vapour. Antoni fastened his jacket to the neck and led Dalton down the road towards the town centre. When they reached a narrow side street, he came to a stop and pointed to it.

"Catherine's bar is up there a little way…at the far end of the street."

Dalton looked surprised. "It is? She told me it was on the river front."

"No. It's up that way. It's not the best location. The tourists don't really explore too far off the main paths. Unless they already know it's there, they won't find it. Last summer, she sent her team around the waterfront, handing out flyers and stuff to drum up trade, but like I say, it's off the beaten track. I'm surprised it's still going, if I'm totally honest."

"We'll find out tonight," Dalton said, cocking an eyebrow at Antoni. "We do still have a date for those cocktails, don't we? You haven't forgotten or changed your mind?"

"I haven't forgotten." He couldn't imagine what Roger would say when he heard he was going out two evenings in a row. Best not to tell him until afterwards. He would only get excited and make a big deal of it.

When they reached the waterfront, the sun shone directly onto the south bank. It was a perfect spring morning. They both put on their sunglasses. Antoni led the way along the marina.

"This is beautiful," Dalton said. "I could almost imagine I'm abroad."

At the Seagull Café, it was warm enough for them to sit at one of the outdoor tables with a prime view of the harbour. Antoni adjusted his chair so the sun was on his back, and he looked straight across at Dalton.

"Now, this is a good location," Dalton said. "Catherine would do much better with a bar down here."

"There's still a lot of competition," Antoni told him. "Just along there is The Lobster Pot. It's a restaurant, but they also have a bar that does premium cocktails. They have proper mixologists who make all the drinks from scratch, play live music on the weekend and every night during the summer. It's hard to beat."

Dalton's breath whistled through his teeth. "Knowing my sister, she won't like that. She's never been good with competition."

"I don't go out much these days, but when I did, The Lobster Pot was my favourite. There's nowhere else like it—not in Nyemouth."

Antoni went inside to place their order—a cappuccino for himself and an americano for Dalton. When he returned, Dalton had relaxed all the way back in his seat, his arms hanging over the sides, his face turned towards the sun. His skin appeared golden in the warm rays. He straightened up when Antoni sat back down.

"I got carried away for a moment, there," Dalton said. "It's like I was in the south of France or somewhere glamourous like that."

"I think the temperatures will be warmer there than you'll find here at the moment."

"How long have you lived here?"

Antoni worked it out on his fingers. "We moved to the UK from Poland when I was five and lived in Darlington until I was around eleven. So, we've been in Nyemouth for around...oh, wow. Twenty-five years."

Dalton's eyebrows rose above his sunglasses. "You must be really attached to the place."

"It hasn't always been easy. There have been issues over the years. My parents suffered terrible racism when we first arrived. It's not perfect now. Roger and me? We still get a bit of trouble from idiots, but this is our home. They won't drive us away. We belong here. I still celebrate our Polish roots with family and friends in the community, but I can barely remember living there. This is my home."

"That pisses me off so much. In this day and age, it's shocking that people have nothing better to do than spread their hate and bigotry."

"They do. It's not as bad as it was for our parents, but I can't say it's ever gone away."

"Antoni, I'm so sorry to hear that."

He shrugged. "It is what it is. We have to deal with it."

Jake Wrangler, co-owner of the café, brought their drinks to the table at that moment. "Hey, Antoni, good to see you again," Jake said, setting the coffee cups in front of them. "It's been a while. How are you doing?"

"I'm okay," Antoni said. Jake had experienced his own troubles while living in Nyemouth and understood better than most people what Antoni had been through.

"I brought you a couple of pieces of shortbread," Jake said, putting a plate on the table between them. "Lizzie baked it fresh this morning. They're still warm." His eyes flicked briefly to Dalton then back to Antoni. He gave an encouraging half-smile. "Enjoy it, guys."

Dalton emptied a sachet of brown sugar into his americano and stirred, before helping himself to one of the generous slabs of shortbread. "These smell amazing."

"They will be. Jake and his sister bake all the cakes, pies and biscuits themselves. Just about everything they sell here is homemade. You should drop by for lunch one day before you go."

"I will. Good food, good coffee, an incredible view and the best company. Seems to me this town has everything."

Antoni busied himself putting sugar in his own coffee. Dalton's constant stream of compliments was disconcerting. He didn't doubt their sincerity, but they were difficult to accept, just the same.

"So, tell me what else you enjoy," Dalton continued. "You've got the gallery, your photographs, great places to eat. What else do you like to do, besides work?"

Antoni spread his hands. "Just regular stuff, really. Nothing exciting. I love to walk—along the cliffs, up the beaches, out on the moors. The coastline is stunning, whichever direction you head. I always take my camera with me, so you could argue that it's still work, but it's what I enjoy. I like to feel the elements against my skin. Even in the depth of winter, I like to feel the cutting winds and squally rain. Other than that, I enjoy cooking. There are a lot of great restaurants here, but none of them cater to traditional Polish food, the stuff my parents make. So, I try to cook the kinds of meals I can't get in town."

Dalton paused, his coffee cup halfway to his lips. "Do you know how perfect that all sounds? It's the kind of lifestyle most of us can only dream of."

"I don't know Surrey. That's where you said you come from, right? I'm sure that it's just as beautiful down there."

"Don't get me wrong, it is. There are some fantastic places about, but I wish I lived on the coast. When you don't have the beaches and cliffs on your doorstep, you tend to forget about them. It's all work and urban living. I try to go running when I can, but more often than not, I end up on the treadmill at the gym rather than getting outside and doing it for real. I've always wanted to get into outdoor pursuits, but there's never been the time. Maybe when I strike the right balance between work life and home, but until then…it's just a dream."

Antoni relaxed as he listened to Dalton talk. The mellifluous tone of his voice put him at ease. "You said last night that you run your own business. I know how difficult that is. Long hours."

He nodded. "There are two of us. My partner, Allegra, is holding down the fort while I'm up here, but you're right. To be successful, we need to put the hours in. We've been going for six years, and we're nowhere near the stage where we can ease up. I keep hoping that by the time we get to ten years, we can take on more staff and reduce our own commitments. We're not there yet." He sipped his coffee. "Still, I shouldn't complain when I enjoy what I do so much."

"And you have your own place?"

He nodded. "Another reason to be grateful. It's mortgaged to the hilt, and it was like living on a building site for three years while I knocked it into shape, but it's mine. It's a good size. I've got a lodger, too—Jack—so I'm not rattling around a big house on my own."

At that moment, Jake shot out the front door, still wearing his kitchen apron. He swerved through the tables and tore along the front of the marina.

"Whoa," Dalton said, sitting up and following Jake's path. "What's his hurry?"

Antoni turned to look, just as the tall front doors of the lifeboat station swung open. Jake disappeared inside.

"An emergency," he said. "Jake is a member of the lifeboat crew. He must have got a call." Another figure ran to the station from the other side and shot through the entrance.

Dalton craned his neck. "Shit. You mean someone is in trouble? Like a fishing boat??"

"Could be. Hopefully it's not that serious. The sea looks calm enough. It could just be a boat that has lost power and needs a tow into the harbour. Sometimes people get cut off by the tide up on North Beach and need rescuing." He couldn't help thinking of that awful night last October when the boat had been launched for a far more serious reason.

Lizzie, Jake's stepsister, came out of the café. She shielded her eyes against the sun with the back of her hand. They watched as the tractor pulled the Atlantic class lifeboat out of the station and down to the water's edge.

"Do you know what they're launching for?" Antoni asked her.

"Apparently, some clothes were found on the beach below North Point this morning," Lizzie said. "They're worried someone might have tried to take their own life, though I don't think there are any witnesses to it, just the pile of clothes. The guys in the boat don't even know who they are looking for. Only that they're women's clothes."

"Oh," Antoni said. "That doesn't sound good. Fingers crossed it's nothing."

Dalton blanched. His face had turned ashen. He sat up straight in his seat. "Shit."

Antoni and Lizzie moved closer.

"What's wrong?"

"Catherine," Dalton said, pulling out his phone. "Her boyfriend called to say she was missing this morning. I didn't think much of it at the time, but *fuck*. She's done this kind of thing before. I'd better check with Justin to see if she's come home yet."

Chapter Six

Dalton called Justin and arranged to meet him at the lifeboat station. He arrived to find a large crowd had gathered on the quay outside, speculating with undisguised excitement about what might have happened. *How strange,* he thought. *Don't they have anything better to do than wait around for bad news?*

The discovery of clothes on the beach had sparked an emergency call to the coastguard and the launch of the lifeboat. Despite all that, he wasn't unduly worried. When he had heard the news himself, his thoughts had turned immediately to Catherine and the conversation he'd had with Justin that morning. Did he believe his sister was the one they were searching for?

Not really.

At least, he didn't believe she was actually missing. Leaving a pile of clothes at the water's edge to make people think she'd gone in? Well, that was classic Catherine. Dalton felt awful thinking about his sister in such a bad light, but he'd been through this kind of thing before. Their entire family had.

"Dalton," a voice behind him said.

In the stark light of day, Justin looked a lot like his photos on Catherine's Instagram account, only more real. His skin, without the aid of filters, was uneven, and he had the tell-tale red blemishes of a heavy drinker around his nose. There were broad shadows under his eyes. Whatever time he'd gone to bed, he would have benefitted from at least another three to four hours of sleep.

"Hey, Justin," Dalton said, trying to sound reassuring.

Justin chewed his fingernails. "What's happening? Any news?"

"Nothing yet. The boat only went out about" – he checked his watch – "twenty-five minutes ago, maybe half an hour."

"Shit. She could have been out there for hours."

Dalton put his arm around him. "Try not to worry. You're jumping to conclusions. Have you tried calling her friends?"

"No one has seen or heard from her since last night."

Something niggled Dalton. *What if she has done something this time?* He quickly steadied himself. *You know her better than that. It's just another trick.*

But what if…?

"Have you reported her missing?" he asked.

Justin's eyes widened. "No. I didn't think it had been long enough. Don't you have to leave it a full day or something like that?"

Dalton gritted his teeth, feeling tension in his jaw. They were being played. He was sure of it. But if Catherine had gone too far, just this once, could he take that risk? "Come on. Let's go inside. We should talk to someone. Let's see if we can discover exactly what they found on that beach."

Dalton pushed through the crowd of onlookers, towards the open door of the station. He spotted an older man wearing a navy-blue polo shirt with the RNLI logo on the chest.

"Excuse me," he said, approaching the man. From his white hair and lined face, he looked to be in his early seventies, but there was a sharpness in his keen blue eyes. "Is there anyone we can talk to about this call out? It's just, well, my sister... We're a little worried."

"What is it, son?" the man asked, his kind voice full of concern.

"She's missing. We *think* she's missing. No one has seen her since last night, and we can't get in touch with her. We heard there had been clothes found on the beach and wondered... Well, you know. Someone said they were women's clothes."

The old man snapped to attention. "Come with me."

He took them to a small office that seemed to double as stockroom for the souvenir shop. Dalton saw the folded black garments on top of the desk when he entered and a pair of black high-heeled sandals.

Fuck.

"These are the items that were handed in," the old man said. "Do you recognise them?"

Dalton hadn't paid too much attention to what Catherine had worn at the party, but the clothes on the desk looked very similar. He turned to Justin and beckoned him forward.

Justin let out a yelp. "They're hers," he gasped.

"Are you sure?" Dalton asked, already certain of the answer.

Justin's bottom lip trembled. "I bought her those shoes especially for the party." He stuffed his fist in his mouth. "She's been going on about them for ages."

The old man was very serious. "Tell me what you can about your sister. Her name, age, everything."

"Catherine Caine," Dalton said. "She's thirty-seven. Long black hair, about five-nine. Slender build."

"Okay, lads, stay here," the man said. "My name is Jacob. I'm going to radio the boat, so they know exactly who they're looking for, then I'm going to get a police officer to speak to you. Okay? They'll need a statement. Just wait here." He left the room.

Justin stood over the desk. He trailed his fingers across the black jacket and trousers. His breath rasped at the back of his throat.

"You're sure you can't remember having an argument last night?" Dalton asked.

"No. Of course not. We never argue."

"Okay," Dalton said, his mind whirling with possibilities. "And everything is fine in your relationship?"

"Of course it is. We love each other. Why are you even asking that? Your sister is missing, for fuck's sake."

Dalton took a deep breath. "Okay. I know this sounds harsh. I'm worried about her, too, but not in the way you think. I'm almost certain that they won't find anything with that boat."

Justin turned on him with narrow eyes. "How can you be so sure?"

Dalton moved closer. He lowered his voice and tried to stay calm. "I don't know how well you know my sister. Have you guys been together long?"

"Since last August."

"Okay. Great. Well, I don't know how much she's told you in that time, or how much you've discovered for yourself, but Catherine is a complicated person. It's not my place to tell you this but, at the moment, I can't see another option." He took a breath. "She's done this kind of thing before. Not *exactly* like this" — he gestured to the pile of clothes — "but similar. Look… She's gone missing several times in the past. She even left notes suggesting she was going to hurt herself."

"I didn't find a note," Justin said defensively.

"That's good. I assume you know she doesn't have a good relationship with the rest of our family, especially our parents. When she was young, she used to fight and argue with our mother all the time. And when she really wanted to get to her, she'd do something like this. One time there was a major police search when she left a note to say she was going to jump off a local viaduct. They searched the riverbanks for miles underneath before she came home three days later. She'd been hiding in an empty trailer the whole time. She said the only reason she returned was because the food she'd stolen had run out."

Dalton leaned against the side of the desk and took another breath. These were difficult stories to share. "Another time, when she was around seventeen, we were on holiday in France. She went missing for three days. That time she hid at the home of a local boy who had fallen under her spell. She did a similar thing when she was at university. Her friends were all worried sick until she turned up a few days later, acting like nothing was wrong."

Justin's lips tightened, and there was a noticeable tic on the left side of his mouth. After a moment he said, "It doesn't mean some harm hasn't come to her today."

"I realise that. I don't have a close relationship with Catherine myself, and as far as I'm aware, she hasn't done anything like this in a long time, but..." He paused, struggling for words in the full glare of Justin's intent scrutiny. He could be way out on this. He didn't know his sister well at all. "You know how you get a feeling about things? About whether they are genuine or not? I just don't get the sense that this is real. It has all the hallmarks of one of her staged disappearances."

"Are you prepared to take the chance on that?"

"No. No, I'm not. The lifeboat crew have to continue with the search, just in case. But I don't think they'll find anything."

Justin's lips curled into a contemptuous sneer. "Then I hope you're right. Because if not, what you're saying now, it's unforgivable."

* * * *

"It's a set-up. She staged the whole thing." Frances Caine's voice was full of angry frustration. "Again."

Dalton sat on a bench at the side of the harbour, talking to his mother on the phone. The lifeboat was still offshore, and a coastguard helicopter had joined them in the search for his sister. Jacob, the kind old guy from the station, had brought a cup of tea and informed him that there was no further news.

Dalton sighed and scratched his head. "Well, obviously, it was staged. The pile of clothes on the beach is proof of that, but it doesn't mean she didn't go into the water. Her boyfriend is genuinely worried."

"Is that any surprise?" his mother said. "She'll have him wrapped around her finger, like every man she's ever met. No one ever knows they're being played until it's too late. You shouldn't fall for it either, Dalton. You know better than anyone what she's capable of."

He sipped the tea. What his mother said was right. Catherine couldn't be trusted. He might be the only member of the family on speaking terms with her these days, but he wasn't naïve. He approached every interaction they had with extreme caution, but that nagging question continued to bother him. What if she had gone through with it? What if she had genuinely harmed herself this time?

"I know," he said. "I get what you're saying. I just can't ignore what's happened."

"Don't you find the timing suspicious?" Frances said. "That she disappears the very night you go to visit her? C'mon, Dalton. You must be able to see what she's up to. She'll have been planning it for weeks. This is the first opportunity she's had to lash out at the family in years, and she hasn't wasted the chance. I knew you shouldn't have gone there. You've walked right into her trap. She's as conniving as ever."

His mother's words were harsh, but he couldn't deny he harboured the same misgivings.

For as long as he could remember, Catherine had bullied her younger brothers, and as the baby, Dalton had borne the brunt of her meanness. One of his earliest memories was of the day she pushed him against a large vase at their grandparent's house. The vase had shattered beneath him, and he remembered lying across his mother's lap crying while the grown-ups plucked pieces of broken china from his bum. Catherine had said it was an accident. He still bore a scar from that day on his left bum cheek.

There were many incidents throughout his childhood he could only remember in fragments —

broken toys, destroyed games, pinching, hair pulling. He used to have a pet budgie, and one day Catherine let the bird out of its cage and opened the window for it to fly away before his eyes.

During his later years, when Catherine went missing and self-harmed, their parents had dismissed her behaviour as attention-seeking, and he had believed them. It was only much later, while at university, that his friends had encouraged him to understand some of her issues and see her through more sympathetic eyes. She was estranged from the rest of the family by that time, and his mother had been furious when she learned Dalton was in touch with her again.

"*She's poison,*" Frances had told him. "*Don't fall for her scheming, son.*"

His mother need not have worried. Though Dalton kept in touch with his sister through texting, social media and birthday cards, they had never been close. It wasn't ideal, but she got on better with him than anyone else. Despite all his reservations, he wanted to believe her — to give her the benefit of the doubt.

"I'm going to hang around a few days, just to be sure. If we're right, and she's true to form, she should be back by the middle of next week."

"What about work? You need to come home for that."

"I wasn't leaving until Monday, anyway. I'll call Allegra later and let her know I'm staying on. I brought my laptop, so I can deal with some of the work from here. It's just a few more days. The hotel isn't full, so it won't be a problem extending my stay."

Frances gave a long sigh down the phone. "I wish you wouldn't. You're playing right into her hands. It's what she wants, you know — to disrupt your life and make it difficult for you."

"Maybe not. Anyway, it doesn't make much difference to me. It's lovely here, so I'll get a chance to look around and explore the area."

"You don't expect that lifeboat to find her today any more than I do. You know this is a con."

"Well, if it is or it isn't, there's clearly something wrong with Catherine. It won't hurt anyone to stay a while and find out what it is."

"Don't be so sure of that. I know she's my daughter, but she's rotten to the core. Everyone who comes into her orbit gets hurt in some way. Don't let it be you, son. She's up to something, that's for certain. Take the utmost care."

Chapter Seven

At the gallery, Antoni found it difficult to focus. He was in no mood to interact with the customers, so withdrew to the stockroom to continue the untaxing job of packing orders for delivery. It was a struggle to think about anything other than Dalton and the strange relationship he had with his sister.

Out of the blue, Dalton had cut short their coffee break and hurried to the lifeboat station when he'd heard a woman's clothes had been found on the beach. No one had seen Catherine since the previous night, and he'd immediately suspected that she might have done something to harm herself.

Suicide, even.

Antoni knew better than anyone not to judge a person by the exterior they presented, but in his dealings with Catherine, she had not seemed the type of woman who would take her own life. Not that it counted for anything, as mental health problems were almost always well concealed. And hadn't Dalton mentioned yesterday that his sister had always suffered from complicated personal issues? It was tragic, whichever way he looked at it. If the abandoned clothes didn't belong to Catherine, then it could be another poor soul who thought life was too difficult to go on with.

Or a hoax. It wasn't out of the question. Leaving clothes on a beach was a classic ruse for someone who wanted to disappear.

But again, Catherine didn't seem the type to pull a vanishing act, especially as she was so focused on being visible for the sake of her followers. The last time he'd looked at her online profile, she seemed to update her status four or five times a day. She thrived on attention, on building her platform. She had nothing to gain by dropping out of sight.

He sighed and placed another print into a cardboard mailbox. What was the point of even dwelling on it? He didn't have the answers, and he had his own problems to worry about.

But there was still Dalton. Antoni liked him, and Dalton appeared to feel the same way. He was certainly forward in letting him know it. He wondered if their cocktail date would go ahead that evening. He hoped so, but it would depend on what happened with Catherine and whether she was really missing or not.

At one o'clock he went back to the gallery floor to relieve Ethan, who was due his lunch break.

The place was busy for so early in the year, and the hour flew by. He sold one of Roger's framed, limited-edition prints for four-hundred-and-fifty pounds, and a lot of their other, less expensive items such as drinks coasters, fridge magnets and postcards. Within the hour, he'd rung in sales of over five-hundred pounds. Pretty good business for mid-March, and it had taken his mind off his prior worries.

Ethan came back at two with a tray carrying three takeaway coffees.

"The lifeboat is still out," he announced, passing the cups around. "They haven't found anything yet, but I heard the clothes have definitely been identified as belonging to Catherine."

Shit. Poor Dalton.

"So they think, what? That she's gone into the water to kill herself?" Roger asked, shaking a sachet of sugar into his drink.

Ethan shrugged. "They must treat it as a worst-case scenario, I guess. There's a helicopter out there, too, as well as the lifeboat. And a news crew have set up outside the station."

Roger grimaced. "Just for once, it would be nice if Nyemouth was featured on TV for a good-news story. They only ever report from here when something goes wrong."

It was a fact the Nowak boys knew too well. Following the murders last autumn and the attack that left Antoni and the writer Christian Costner seriously wounded, the press had descended in a swarm. Roger had had to face the worst of it. When Antoni was laid up in hospital, they had pestered his brother for inside knowledge on the murders. Even afterwards, when Antoni was recuperating at Roger's, one photographer had persuaded a resident in one of the houses out of the back to let them use a long-distance lens to capture pictures of him through the windows.

And now they were back. The potential suicide of a social media influencer would have them salivating all over again.

Antoni wondered whether Dalton was prepared for what was to come. Maybe there was some way of warning him.

"This is going to sound awful," Ethan said, lowering his voice so the customers wouldn't hear him, "but if anything has happened to her, I don't think many people round here will miss her."

Roger huffed. "Well, we will. She hasn't settled her bill."

Antoni cuffed his shoulder. "Guys, c'mon. Have a bit of respect."

Ethan raised his hands. "I'm just saying what everyone is thinking. You'll struggle to find anyone with a good word to say about Catherine Caine. And you can take that from me, the idiot who used to work for her."

"How long did you work at White Lady?" Antoni asked.

"Too long. About six weeks, maybe less. I've tried to block it from my mind."

Roger laughed. "It was that bad?"

Ethan screwed up his face. "*Worse*. It was horrible. She has such a high turnover of staff. If I did last six weeks, then it will have been longer than most. She was the worst boss I've ever had. Everyone said the same thing."

Antoni had heard Ethan make similar statements before, but now his interest was piqued as to why. "What did she do so wrong?"

"She was a bully, for a start. She treated her staff like dirt. Expected them to work overtime at no notice, but also cut the hours without explanation for the people she didn't like. She was always belittling the staff in front of customers. I remember one night she was blue in the face from screaming at me before the whole bar. She thought I'd made a mistake with one of the orders. When the customers corrected her and explained there had been no mistake, she stormed off. There was no apology for that or anything else. And our pay was never right. We were always getting short-changed on the wages, and she took charge of sharing out the tips, taking the biggest cut for herself."

"Wow," Roger said. "A real Cruella Deville."

"That's not the worst of it. She was physical, too. I saw her throw a bottle at someone who irritated her. Another guy who worked there told me she felt him up and threatened to sack him if he didn't go down on her. He had a girlfriend and wasn't interested. He packed the job in rather than face her again."

"Whoa," Antoni said. "How come no one reported this? They could have had her arrested."

"I've no idea. She's quite formidable. Maybe they didn't think it was worth the effort. It's not as if anyone actually liked working there, so no one was desperate to get their job back after they left. Also, I don't think she appreciated the damage that word-of-mouth could do. Everyone who worked there went away and told all the people they knew how awful it was. The business is going down the pan. I'm surprised it's still open, to be honest, though she does have that rich boyfriend now, so maybe he's bankrolling the bar. Either that, or her disappearance is an insurance job."

Strange, Antoni thought, *how no one really believes she has hurt herself.*

Catherine Caine thought she was a beloved influencer. That might be the case online, but in reality, no one seemed to like her.

He wondered what Dalton thought. Was he taking it seriously or did he believe it was a PR stunt too?

Antoni was conflicted all over again. As much as he liked Dalton, did he really want to involve himself in another messy media story?

Perhaps the best thing for the sake of his own wellbeing would be to keep far away from this.

Chapter Eight

Justin grew increasingly restless as the afternoon wore on and there was no further news of Catherine. The lifeboat continued its search along the coast and updated the crew at the station over the radio.

"It's hopeless," he said, smoking his fourth consecutive cigarette. "No one can survive in the water for this long, not with temperatures like they are. It's March, for Christ's sake. We're barely out of winter."

Dalton had done his best to placate him, but there were only so many cups of tea he could provide. They stood at the front of the station. Thankfully, most of the crowd that had gathered earlier to gawp had gotten bored and moved away.

The police had also been and gone, having filed a missing person report and taken statements from each of them.

Justin could not be swayed from his way of thinking and was convinced Catherine had gone into the sea to take her own life. It was an idea Dalton still struggled to accept. His mother wasn't the best gauge when it came to his sister's behaviour, but he couldn't get past the notion that this was nothing more than a bit of cynical and cruel manipulation. Who was being manipulated? He wasn't sure. It could be him but was more likely to be Justin. He was far more emotionally invested in Catherine than anyone else in her life at the moment.

If she were playing one of her heartless tricks, Justin was the one who would hurt the most.

"Listen," Dalton said. "Instead of waiting around here for news from the crew, why don't we do something more productive?"

"Like what?" Justin asked, gripping the butt of a cigarette between his thumb and first finger.

"You said she doesn't live with you. That she still has her own flat."

He shook his head and sneered. "Don't you think I've already checked there?"

"That was this morning," Dalton said kindly. "Let's look again. Even if she's not there, we might find something you missed. You were in a hurry earlier. We can take our time now."

"I want to wait here, in case there's news."

"We're not going far," Dalton persisted. "I'll leave my number with Jacob. He'll call us as soon as he hears anything."

After further persuasion, Justin agreed. "We can walk from here. It's not far."

They headed across the bridge, past Quay House and back along the waterfront on the opposite side. There were a lot of fishing boats moored in the harbour. Huge working trawlers and sleek pleasure boats nestled for space alongside yachts and tourist vessels offering coastal cruises and sunset trips. There were several amusement arcades and lots of cafés, bars and bistros. He even noticed an old-fashioned, 1950s style ice cream parlour.

Dalton found it strange to imagine his sister ending up in a place like this. For years she had boasted of her jet-set lifestyle and cosmopolitan existence. She'd even spent three years living in Spain as the fiancé of an international football star, where her life had been a catalogue of parties and holidays. At least it had seemed that way from her posts.

How did she end up in a small, seaside town on the Northeast coast of England?

Nyemouth was beautiful, he couldn't deny it, but it wasn't very Catherine Caine.

Had she really changed that much? Perhaps she was no longer the person he thought she was.

"This way," Justin said, leading him to a narrow path between a pub and a restaurant.

They climbed a steep set of steps, where the stone was so old it was worn down in the centre. At the top, the path widened into a broad street. The road curved to the right, and they were on a street of four- and five-storey townhouses. Most of them were in business as hotels and guest houses, though some had been converted into holiday apartments.

Justin stopped in front of one of the buildings, and they climbed more stone steps to the front door.

"Catherine lives down there." He pointed to the below-ground basement level. He pulled out a bunch of keys, selected the right one and opened the front door to a beautiful hallway with a pale oak floor.

They took the stairs to the basement.

It was an amazing old building, restored to the highest standard, but again, it didn't seem like the kind of place his sister would choose to live.

The door opened into a small hallway. A massive, framed photograph of Catherine occupied the opposite wall.

This is more like it, he thought. *She'll fit right in here.*

Justin froze in front of him, and Dalton walked straight into his back.

"Oh, sorry," he said, stepping away. "What is it?"

Then he heard it for himself. Noise ahead of them.

There was someone in the apartment.

Justin rushed forward. "Catherine."

Dalton hurried after him, into a sparse open-plan living and dining room. There were more pictures of Catherine on the walls.

"Catherine, are you here?" Justin hurried towards a door across the room.

It opened before he reached it and a slender woman dressed in black trousers and a cream top, stepped through.

"It's just me," she said in a flat, emotionless voice.

With her tawny blonde hair and pretty, girl-next-door looks, there was something familiar about her. Dalton couldn't recall meeting her at the party, but she could have been there.

Justin faltered and his shoulders sagged. "What are *you* doing here?"

The woman crossed the room and put her small purse on top of the counter. "The same as you, I expect. Looking for anything that might help."

"Did you find anything?"

She frowned and swept her hair away from her face. "Nothing." She caught sight of Dalton and gave an uncertain smile.

"Hello," he said. "I'm Dalton, Catherine's brother."

"Hi. Yes, I know who *you* are." Her attention returned to Justin. "Any news?"

He shook his head.

"Her bed hasn't been slept in," the woman said, jerking her head towards the door she had just come through.

"Of course, it hasn't. She was with me last night," Justin snapped.

He's close to losing it.

"All right, keep your hair on," the woman said. "I'm trying to be helpful. Jesus."

Dalton stepped forward. "Excuse me. But who are *you*?"

She put one hand on the countertop and the other on her hip, staring him out. "I'm Larissa," she said, as though it should be obvious. "I'm Catherine's friend."

"Okay," he said.

"You must recognise me. #LarissaBakes. On Insta. That's my handle. I'm also on YouTube and Tik Tok." When the announcement had no effect, she continued. "I do cupcakes and yummy treats. All the top chefs follow me. Some of them have even stolen my ideas. Anyway, I'm also on tonnes of Catherine's posts. We hashtag each other. People think we influencers all hate each other, but it's so untrue. Catherine and I have each other's backs."

It struck him that Larissa was as shallow as the things she said. Catherine had never been into baking or those fancy cupcakes that looked one-hundred-percent nicer than they ever tasted. Had the world of social media and celebrity really changed her that much? More likely she would latch on to any popular trend.

"How did you get in?" he asked her.

"I have my own key — and the alarm code," she stated. "It's what friends do for each other, in case of an emergency. If anything happened to me, Catherine has the keys to my place to be able to feed my fur babies."

Now she really was talking about another person. Catherine loathed pets of any kind, and from Dalton's experience, animals were not keen on her, either.

"I take it you haven't heard from her today," he said.

"No. Why do you think I'm here?"

"Dalton thinks Catherine is playing us for fools," Justin said flatly. "That she staged her disappearance to wind me up."

Larissa's eyes narrowed. "You are fucking joking, right?"

"I never said she was playing you," Dalton said, keeping his tone even and calm. "But she's done this before...several times. And she always came home after a few days."

"Bullshit," Larissa snarled. "Jesus, she was right about you a lot, wasn't she? Her whole family are fucking monsters. She told us what you were all like. No wonder she moved up here to get away from you. You're sick, man. Really sick to come out with shit like that while the lifeboat is out there now searching for her."

Suddenly Larissa and Catherine's friendship made sense. Apart from their influencing careers, they shared a temper that could go from zero to a hundred in a second.

"I'm not ruling anything out. My sister is a complicated person. But I'm not going to jump to the worst conclusion. I've been there before—me and the shitty family you think so little of. And every one of those times, after days of stress, worry, not to mention huge expense to the emergency services, she came home without apology or much explanation."

"She's never run away in the time I've known her," Justin said.

"With every respect, that's only been six months," Dalton said.

"Well, I've known her a lot longer than that," Larissa said, "and she's never done this before. Maybe her disappearance has something to do with you. Ever thought of that? That seeing someone from her toxic family after all this time might have triggered a trauma she's spent years trying to get over?" Larissa stood with both hands on her hips now, gloating as she stared him down.

These people are way too highly strung, he thought. It was time to go.

"I'll be at the hotel for a few more days if you need me," he said to Justin, refusing to rise to Larissa's provocation. "And I'll check in at the lifeboat station later for an update. I know you don't want to hear it right now, but it will do everyone good to stop worrying so much. Catherine will come home. I'm sure of it."

Larissa continued to swear at him as he headed for the door. Dalton tuned out most of what she said.

Catherine had a knack of pushing people's buttons and dialling their emotions up to ten. It was clear she had done it to her boyfriend and Larissa. After thirty-one years as her brother, Dalton realised he was finally immune to it.

The new people in his sister's life were already stressed to death about her disappearance, but he would wait until there was further news before pushing the panic button. Until then, he intended to calm down and continue his day as planned—which hopefully meant he still had a date with Antoni.

Chapter Nine

It was after eight when Dalton left the hotel to find his sister's bar on the other side of the river. There was still no news on Catherine. The lifeboat and the coastguard had ceased their search, having found nothing. A police officer had called him around six, but it was only to ask more questions about his sister's state of mind and enquire whether he had heard from other family members who might have seen or had contact from her. There was an inevitable sense of déjà vu about the whole day, stoking childhood memories of his parents talking to the police during one of Catherine's disappearances.

His father also called as he was about to set off to meet Antoni. Dalton had assured him that he would get in touch as soon as he had anything to report.

There was a sad sense of weary expectation in his dad's voice, and Dalton realised he was far from alone in his scepticism. He'd been quite shaken after the outburst from Larissa earlier in the day. He wished he could share the concern Justin and Larissa obviously felt, but there was no point in pretending. He didn't.

His instinct stayed the same. This was an elaborate hoax. They might never find out why, but he felt more certain of it with every minute she was away.

Dalton crossed the bridge with his hands in his pockets and his shoulders slumped. He should be on a high, heading out for a date with a great, sexy, interesting guy. Why had he thought it was a good idea to meet at Catherine's bar out of all the places in Nyemouth? Hopefully, they could move on once he'd settled his curiosity.

He found the alley Antoni had shown him earlier. It was another narrow street, with old buildings towering on either side. The pavement inclined at a steep angle as he followed it away from the harbour area.

White Lady was the only bar at the top of the street, a fair trek from the touristy attractions of the marina. Dalton was slightly out of breath when he opened the door and stepped inside.

The interior was exactly how he had imagined — lots of dark glass, polished metal, white Grecian pillars and sharp angles. There was a small dance floor at the back, empty as a DJ played a generic, mid-tempo dance track. Trendy, but it would never attract anyone to the floor at this time in the evening. He wouldn't be surprised if he was some hip DJ, used to playing to pumped up city crowds. No doubt he had cost a fortune.

The place was almost empty. As he looked around, he spotted Antoni standing at a tall table by the window. He waved him over.

Dalton's mood brightened in an instant. Something tugged at his insides, like an undercurrent, and he felt happy for the first time in hours.

"I'm sorry I'm late. My phone has been ringing all evening. I couldn't get away."

"You're not that late," Antoni answered with a shy smile. "Have you had any news?"

"Nothing. I don't expect we will now. Three to five days... That's been Catherine's usual timescale in the past. We won't hear anything until Monday at the earliest."

"You seem very sure of that. Aren't you worried at all?"

"There are moments when I think I ought to be. Like...she's my sister. I should be concerned, right? But I just don't feel it." He thumped his abdomen. "In here. I don't buy it."

Antoni nodded and gave one of his sad, haunting smiles. "I hope you're right."

"Let me get us some drinks. I need to think about something else for a while. What will you have?"

Antoni brandished the bar menu. "It's two for one on the cocktails. Maybe this is what you need to cheer you up?"

"It's as good a place to start as any. Is there anything you have your eye on?"

"An espresso martini sounds good."

"It does. And could be just the pickup I need. I'll order and be right back."

As he crossed the room to the bar, Dalton counted nine other customers scattered about the place. Hardly packed for a Saturday evening. If Catherine was the big social media influencer she claimed to be, surely her name alone could draw a weekend crowd at least. *Not from the evidence of this*.

There were no other customers waiting to be served. The two bartenders looked bored and set about mixing the order together. Dalton caught snatches of their conversation above the dull music.

"I don't think anyone will miss her…"

"…got an interview at a new place in Morpeth on Wednesday. I've been looking to get out of here for ages…"

"If you leave, I'm going too… There's no way I'm staying here, especially not if she does come back…"

He didn't want to embarrass them by revealing who he was, but it was obvious the people who worked for Catherine had little love for her. The more he learned about his sister's life, the stranger it became—her relationship with Justin, friendship with Larissa, a failing business. Not that it should surprise him. He'd known her all his life, and she had never been the conventional type.

Antoni was looking at his phone but stuffed it in his back pocket when Dalton returned with the drinks.

"You look nice," Dalton told him, admiring his appearance.

"I do?"

"Of course you do. But a little different. Did you cut your hair?"

Antoni brushed his fingers self-consciously through his hair, then fiddled with his right ear. "Oh, no. I had a shower about half an hour ago. I washed it. That's all."

"It looks nice," Dalton said. Antoni actually looked smoking hot, but Dalton had quickly come to realise that compliments embarrassed him, so he kept them understated.

Antoni wore a navy jersey top that skimmed his slim torso, and washed-out jeans. Antoni met his eyes briefly before focusing on his cocktail and taking a sip.

Dalton did the same, hoping the alcohol would relax Antoni.

"Mmm. It's good."

Antoni nodded. "I don't think anyone has ever complained about the quality of drinks here. I think it's more the location and lack of atmosphere. Also, outside of happy hour, this place is *really* expensive. Tourists might pay those prices, but the locals are a lot more careful with their money."

"That's typical of my sister. She has created the kind of bar *she* wants to sit in, rather than what will appeal to a wider audience. I don't think the staff are too happy here, either." Dalton told him what he'd overheard at the bar.

"That doesn't surprise me. Ethan, our assistant at the gallery, you met him briefly this morning? He used to work here."

"Don't tell me. He hated it, too."

Antoni gave a cute grimace. "Sorry...but yes. He didn't like to work for your sister at all. I don't think it's a very supportive or friendly environment."

"Does Catherine actually run this bar?"

"No. I'm sure there's a manager, but I think she keeps a firm hand on things. Ethan was pleased to get out."

"Wow. Poor kid. That sucks." He took another sip. "You know what? This is going to sound heartless, but I've had enough of talking about my sister today. It feels like she's taken over my entire life."

"But she's missing. Despite everything, you must be worried about her."

Dalton shrugged. "I think she's going to walk back in a day or two, so let's not allow her to take up another minute of this evening. I came here to be with you, not her. I want to get to know you and find out more about you."

"Like what? I think I've told you everything."

Dalton reached across the table and ran his fingertips over the back of Antoni's hand. Antoni flinched slightly, but didn't pull away, and after a moment, he moved his hand a fraction closer to Dalton's. Dalton trailed his fingers towards Antoni's wrist, grazing the dark hair on the back of his hand.

"You've barely told me anything," he said softly. "You don't like talking about yourself. I've noticed the way you change the subject whenever I try. But I'm here for you. Tell me as much as you feel comfortable with."

Antoni took another drink and rasped his fingers across his stubble for a moment. "You're right, I don't like talking about myself. Why don't you ask me something instead and let me answer?"

"Okay." Dalton edged around the table, getting closer to him. He could smell the freshness of Antoni's skin and recently shampooed hair. "Well, I guess what I really want to know is, are you single? Is there anyone around who might be pissed off with me for flirting with you?"

Antoni smiled, and the corners of his eyes creased in the most adorable way. The sight caused Dalton's weary heart to brighten.

"There's no one else. I've been single for over a year. I was in a long-term relationship before that...for almost three years. My ex, Harry, is with someone else now, and we are all good friends, so there are no complications in that way."

"Excellent." Dalton grinned. "But how come you've been on your own for so long? Are the guys around here all blind?"

Antoni peeked at him then looked away. His voice flattened. "It's complicated. And...well, perhaps later, I'll be able to tell you. Somewhere quieter...maybe."

Dalton had suspected there was a backstory to Antoni. He was so forlorn and introspective, when a man like him—sexy, successful—should be on top of the world. From the outside, he appeared to have it all—a thriving career, his own business, a supportive family—but something had caused the sadness behind those lovely grey eyes. If he got on so well with his ex-boyfriend, then that was unlikely to be the reason, but something haunted him. Dalton knew not to press it. Antoni would tell him if, and when, he was ready to.

"So, what is it like?" Dalton asked. "In Nyemouth, I mean. It seems great to me, but don't all holiday destinations? What's it like living here all year round?"

Antoni's confidence returned now that he was on a safe subject. He told Dalton about the local Polish community and the support he received from them. He talked about his love for the beaches, moors and cliffs of Northumberland. "Even in the winter, when it's blowing a gale and the rain is belting down, I still love it. It's wild and untamed. It's a sense of nature you can never experience in a busy town or a city. I once went with Roger and a group of friends on a five-night trip to Las Vegas. I spent weeks and months planning and looking forward to it, and when we got there, I hated every minute. All that noise and light and everything built up to the heavens? It was awful. I couldn't wait to get home."

"It would be a dull world if everyone liked the same things."

"You would find Nyemouth boring," Antoni said. "I'm sure of it."

Is he serious? "After all that's happened in the last twenty-four hours, 'boring' is the last word I would use for this town. If it keeps up, I'll need to go home for a rest from it all."

Antoni gave another of those delightful smiles that crinkled his eyes and melted Dalton's heart. He wondered again how such a gorgeous man could be so lacking in confidence.

"Come on," Dalton said when they had finished their drinks. "I've had more than enough of White Lady. Why don't you show me what else the town has to offer?"

"Okay. Though I'm not sure what you expect me to know. I hardly go out, and I avoid the bars at weekends with a passion."

Dalton gently brushed his fingers against Antoni's as they stepped outside. "You'll be safe with me, I promise."

The comment was met with a strange silence. Antoni didn't speak again as they walked down the narrow path, pulling ahead when there was no room for them to walk side by side, and Dalton wondered if he had said something wrong.

When they reached the main road, Antoni spoke. "There are two ways we can go from here. Over there is The Lobster Pot. It's mainly a restaurant, but they have a cocktail bar, too. It will be much busier than your sister's place. Or in that direction is The Fisherman's Arms. It's a pub, right on the harbour. More traditional."

"The pub sounds great," Dalton said. "One cocktail is enough for me."

The evening was surprisingly cold, and Dalton was glad he'd brought a jacket, pulling the collar around his neck as Antoni led him to the pub he'd noticed earlier, close to the lifeboat station. The station was in darkness with the tall front doors fastened shut. The search for Catherine had been called off at dusk.

Antoni told him to get them a table while he went for the drinks. Dalton chose a quiet corner, away from the dining room and the busy bar area. The pub was a world away from White Lady and a lot busier. Even out of season, he estimated they were at seventy to eighty percent capacity. Whatever Catherine was doing with her bar, it was all wrong. It lacked the warmth and hospitality of this place.

Antoni returned with a white wine for Dalton and a beer for himself. He put a menu on the table. "I don't know if you've eaten today, but the food is very good here."

Dalton realised he hadn't had anything since breakfast time. "Shit, you're right. I haven't. What about you? I don't want to eat if you're not."

"I haven't had anything, either. I hadn't even thought about food until we arrived."

Dalton was surprised to find a substantial vegetarian selection. "Wow. It's nice to see something more than pasta and tomato sauce on offer."

"Do you mind if I order something non-vegetarian?" Antoni asked.

Dalton's heart warmed to him even further. "Of course I don't mind. You have what you like, and don't mind me. It's my choice not to eat meat, but I don't expect anyone to abstain on my behalf. Knock yourself out."

There was so much to choose from, but Dalton eventually opted for a niçoise salad with grilled halloumi in place of the traditional tuna. Antoni went for the house special of fish and chips. When it arrived, the food was delicious. Antoni relaxed further as they ate and drank, telling him what little he could remember of his childhood in Poland and his life in the UK.

To Dalton, it sounded idyllic compared to the relative chaos of his own upbringing.

Antoni turned out to be an avid amateur cook. "It started as a necessity," he explained over their third drink. "It's just about impossible to get Polish food in cafés and restaurants here in the UK, as I've told you, so the people of our community keep our traditions alive. I used to help my mother prepare great pots of food for the monthly social clubs, and my interest in cooking grew from there."

"Is that what you cook? Polish recipes?"

"Not always. I like a variety of things, but I suppose, yes, I do have a large repertoire of Polish dishes." He laughed and, for once, seemed quite unselfconscious.

"I'd love to try it sometime. I don't think I'm familiar with anything of that sort."

"That's no surprise. Like I said, it's hard to find in this country."

Antoni was the cutest, most natural guy Dalton had met in a long time, maybe ever. The more time he spent with him, just talking and enjoying his company, the stronger his attraction grew. Why were there no men like this closer to home? Why did he have to travel to the opposite end of the country to meet him?

As Antoni spoke, Dalton became fascinated by his mouth. His eyes were drawn to his wide lips and the way they articulated his words.

The urge to kiss him became overwhelming.

Was he reading the signs right? He was certain Antoni was into him. Maybe not as much as Dalton liked him, but the vibes were definitely there.

Emboldened by alcohol and desire, Dalton reached across the table and took his hand, linking fingers with him. He knew in a second that he had made a mistake. Antoni's whole body stiffened.

Shit! Judged it all wrong. Antoni had told him this morning that he was uncomfortable with uninvited physical contact. *Idiot!*

Dalton withdrew. "Sorry. I'm *very* sorry. I shouldn't have done that." He sat all the way back in his seat. His heart pounded in his chest. *I've blown it.*

Antoni chewed his bottom lip and seemed to have trouble getting himself together.

Oh no, Dalton thought. *He's going to leave.*

Antoni put both hands on the table and looked down at them. He took a breath and kept his eyes lowered as he spoke. "It's not that I don't like you. We only met last night, but I feel... Well, I don't know what it is I feel, but it's something. I'm not rejecting you. It's just... I find it hard when people I don't know touch me."

Dalton cursed himself. He was so used to his family and friends with their hugs and cuddles, he often forgot that other people weren't so open. "Antoni, I'm truly mortified. I should have had more respect for your personal space."

Antoni looked up. His eyes were wet.

Oh, no. I've fucked this up big time.

"It's not your fault," Antoni said. "I'm the one who has issues."

"Don't blame yourself. Please. It's me who's in the wrong."

Antoni took another deep breath. "Look... There's a reason I'm like this." His voice trembled. He was clearly trying to stop those tears from falling over his eyelids. "I'd like to tell you. If you are seriously interested in me —"

"I am," Dalton blurted.

After a long pause, Antoni said, "I can't do it here. If we go somewhere quiet, I'll explain."

Dalton nodded. He'd agree to anything Antoni asked to make him feel comfortable. "You know the town, I don't. We can go wherever you want. It's up to you."

Antoni exhaled and seemed to relax a tiny bit. "Okay. Let's finish here and go. Then I'll tell you everything."

Chapter Ten

Antoni's hand shook as he tried to get the key into the lock of his front door. It took three attempts to insert it.

What the hell am I doing? Bringing home a man I barely know.

For six months, he had taken every precaution. He'd been guarded and defensive, keeping everyone but those closest to him at a distance, and now he was about to throw it all away, to risk everything, for the sake of a charming stranger.

He hesitated. *Do I turn the key or not? It's not too late to get out of this.*

"Are you okay?" Dalton asked.

His voice was kind and his features, which glowed in the streetlight, showed concern.

"I'm fine. Yes." Antoni opened the door before he changed his mind. He turned on the light and led the way. The stairs creaked beneath his feet. "Mind your head. The building is old and some of the ceilings are low." He demonstrated by ducking beneath the overhang halfway up.

From the landing, he opened the door to the living room and turned on three antique lamps before closing the curtains.

"Wow. Cool place," Dalton said, following him into the room.

"Like I said, it's very old. Roger thinks I should renovate and modernise. He would gut the place if I let him, but I like it like this." Antoni had sought to retain the original features, and all the upgrades he had made had been sympathetic to the style of the flat. Most of his furniture was also old — stuff he had reclaimed or acquired from second hand shops and reupholstered for comfort. The creaky floorboards and narrow staircase were all part of the charm of living in the historic end of Nyemouth.

Looking at Dalton standing in the middle of the living room, Antoni realised he was the first person to come back to the flat, apart from family members, since Harry. He was the first man he'd been alone with since they had split, over a year ago.

"Have a seat," he said. "I'll get us some drinks. All I have is vodka…if that's okay."

Dalton nodded. "Perfect."

"How would you like it?"

"I don't mind — cola, lemonade, tonic. Whatever you have in."

"I won't be long. Make yourself at home. Put on some music or the TV if you'd like some noise."

Antoni's mouth was bone dry when he reached the kitchen. He ran the cold tap and drank two full glasses of water.

Where is this going? Where do I want it to go?

Dalton hadn't asked to come back to the flat. It had been Antoni's idea. That had to imply that he wanted to take things further. But what else could he have done? There had been few other options. If he were going to be honest and tell his story, he couldn't have done it in any of the town-centre bars, and the night was too cold for a heart to heart along the waterfront, which left Dalton's hotel or here. Bringing Dalton home had triggered his anxiety, but Antoni felt more in control in his own environment than anywhere else.

We're here now. There was no point delaying. He had to get on with it and do what he intended.

He got another glass for Dalton and filled both with ice before taking the bottle of vodka out of the freezer. He splashed a good measure into each glass and took them back to the living room with a bottle of Coke so Dalton could add his own mixer.

Dalton was hunkered over his record boxes, flipping through Antoni's vinyl collection. The position caused his trousers to ride down at the rear and gave a flash of his fuzzy bum crack. The sight sparked a surge of arousal. He hadn't seen a naked man since Harry, either, and that strip of exposed flesh was intensely erotic.

"You've got an amazing collection here." Dalton glanced over his shoulder. "All these old movie soundtracks... Is that what you're into?"

Antoni sat their drinks on the grey marble coasters he had picked up at a Sunday morning market in Newcastle. "Yes. I like the atmosphere of a good soundtrack. And it's great music to work to. There are no songs to distract me."

"I never thought of that." Dalton examined the sleeve for *Vertigo.* "I'm a streamer through and through. Usually too lazy to even pick my own music, so I just put a playlist on. You know, one for running, one for the gym, another for lazing around. But this is much cooler. Are these all originals?"

Antoni stole another sneaky peek at his bum crack. "Some are. Others are modern reissues. To be honest, the newer releases sound a lot better than some of the old ones."

"Even still, some of these must be worth a fortune." He picked up the soundtrack for *Jaws 2*.

"Maybe from a record trader." Antoni laughed. "I found nearly all of those in charity shops and car boot sales. I don't think I paid more than a fiver for any of them."

Talking about his records had broken the ice. He sat in his favourite armchair, no longer daunted by Dalton's presence in his home. He picked up his vodka and took a long sip of the thick, icy liquor, relaxing further.

Dalton rose, hitched up his trousers, and moved to the sofa. Antoni concealed his disappointment—*that looked like a glorious backside*—and indicated his drink.

"Are you having it neat?" Dalton asked, splashing Coke onto his own glass.

"It's the only way. It's a crime to spoil good vodka with a syrupy mixer."

Dalton flashed his cheeky smile. "You're far more sophisticated than I am, with your vinyl and your vodka. I'm just a peasant with my playlists and cola-y drinks. Cheers, anyway." He raised his glass and winked.

"Cheers," Antoni said, saluting with his own glass.

Dalton smacked his lips appreciatively. "Mmm. This is good." He looked at the bottle on the coffee table.

"*Gold filtered vodka.* Man, you don't mess about, do you?"

Antoni shrugged. "I guess life is too short to waste it on crap. I know what I like, and if I can afford it, I treat myself."

"I love your attitude." Dalton took another drink and looked at him earnestly. "Does this have anything to do with what you want to tell me?"

Antoni gave a light snort through his nose. "You're perceptive." He took a moment to gather his thoughts. It was the thing he hated talking about the most. The PTSD counsellor he saw every fortnight had tried all kinds of ways to make it easier for him, but it didn't get any better. How fucked up that he struggled to be open with the woman he'd been visiting for the last four months but was about to tell all to a relative stranger. "You're right. There's something about me you should know before we go any further – *if* we're to go any further."

Dalton shuffled across the sofa, coming nearer to him. "I'm listening. But only tell me what you want to."

He took another hit of vodka to steel himself. "Okay." A deep breath. "So, you can't have failed to notice that I'm socially awkward. Going to those bars tonight, even with you, was a struggle. But I wasn't always like that. I wasn't always like this. There was a time when I loved going out. I had loads of friends, and we'd catch up three or four nights a week. A lot of the time, I only came home to change my clothes before going out again. That was the kind of man I was until last October." His mouth was dry again. He licked his lips and looked Dalton straight in the eyes. "Did you hear anything about the murders here in Nyemouth last year?"

Dalton's eyes widened. "Murders? No. Shit. I'm sorry. I'm lousy about following the news. It's so depressing and stressful, so I tend to tune out. So, what are you telling me? You were caught up in it somehow?"

It seemed like there was a frightened bird fluttering in his chest, desperate to get out. "I'd rather not go into the details. You can read it all online. There was plenty written about the case. But yes, three young men were murdered here last October."

"You knew them? Right?"

Antoni nodded. "I knew two of the victims. I knew their killer, too. He had no intention of stopping at three murders. He attacked another two men before it was over. But they were lucky. They survived." He swallowed. "And I was one of them."

"Oh my God, Antoni." Dalton crouched forward on the sofa. "I'm so sorry. I don't know what else to say. I can't imagine what...what that was like."

"I was stabbed in the belly." The words sounded cold, distant, as if they were coming from someone else. "It wasn't far from here, actually — just down the road, at the entrance to South Pier. One good jab of the knife into the guts... He left me for dead, while he went after my ex, Harry."

"Was Harry the second survivor?"

He nodded. "I would have died right there if Harry's new boyfriend, Christian, hadn't come along. He called for an ambulance and went after them. Christian also got a knife to the belly for his trouble. It was" — he blew out a long breath, whiffling his lips like a horse, and spread his arms — "awful, like living through a nightmare or a scene from a horror movie."

"How bad were your injuries?"

"I had to have surgery on my abdomen." He brushed his fingers across his torso, indicating the area. "Thankfully, I made a full recovery—physically, at least. I've got a dramatic scar, but no permanent damage."

"And Christian?"

"He's the same. He seems fine now. Actually, he seems pretty normal. I don't think it affected him in the same way as it did me"—he tapped his forehead—"in here. Christian is a journalist and more used to dealing with stories like this."

"Hey, don't be hard on yourself. Anyone would be the same if they went through what you did. I take it they caught the bastard?"

"He's missing," Antoni said coldly, "at sea. His body was never found, but there was a hell of a storm that night. There's no way he could have survived. The sea will have carried him miles out."

"Okay." Dalton nodded slowly. He took a drink and stared into the depths of his glass before returning his gaze to Antoni. "So, how are you now?"

Good question. How am I now?

"I'm really not sure. Getting better, I guess. It's only recently that I returned to work and moved back here. I was living with Roger. He didn't want me to move out, but I needed my own space again. So that's a kind of progress, right? Small steps, at least."

"Sounds like massive progress to me."

He shrugged. "It's still not easy. I can't remember the last time I had a good night's sleep. I get three or four broken hours most nights. When I do sleep, I have the worst dreams—not always about what happened—but dark, nasty stuff that must be connected. My appetite is shot. If I hadn't gone with you for the meal this evening, I might have eaten a slice of toast or had half a tin of soup. I've lost a lot of weight. I used to be more like you, you know, in size and build. I try to eat, but it's hard to muster much interest. And before all this, I loved food."

"I thought you said you enjoy cooking."

"I do. It's one of the things that helps me to relax. But I give most of what I make to Roger and Ethan. I pretend it's what I have left over, but it's usually everything I cooked." Antoni caught himself and gasped.

"What is it?"

"I... I'm, er, shocked that I'm telling you all this. My own family don't even know most of it."

"I suspect they do…subconsciously, at least."

"I know. But I haven't told anyone. Only you."

Dalton put his hand on the edge of Antoni's armchair. Antoni realised he was holding back from touching him after his earlier rejection in the pub. "I'm honoured that you have."

"I shouldn't burden you with my problems, not after everything you've had to deal with today."

"Are you kidding? I'm much more interested in you than anything my flaky sister has been up to."

Antoni winced. "You shouldn't talk like that—not until you know she's safe."

"She's fine. Trust me. I'm sure of it. And I mean what I said. I'm honoured you chose me to open up to."

Antoni snatched the vodka bottle from the table and splashed another loose measure over his ice. In a strange way, it did feel good to talk to Dalton, maybe because he was a stranger and hadn't been there at the time of the murders. The thing he found most difficult when talking to anyone from Nyemouth was the sympathy they exuded. He didn't want it or need it. Most people were well-meaning, but they had no idea how hard it was for him to stand there and wither beneath their kindly gazes.

"Am I right in thinking that your ordeal is the reason you don't like people to touch you?" Dalton asked.

He nodded. "I was never a touchy-feely kind of person before, but I find unsolicited contact even more difficult now."

"I'm so sorry. God, I'm an idiot. You should have told me to back the fuck off."

Antoni chuckled. "That's not the kind of thing I would say to anyone."

Dalton grinned. "That's because you're too nice."

"I just need a little warning, that's all. I know I have a problem with intimacy and personal space, but I'm working on getting better. I try not to flinch when anyone comes near, but often, I can't control it."

"We're all too touchy-feely these days, anyway. It's the rest of us who need to calm the fuck down, rather than assume everyone we meet wants our damn physical contact."

Antoni laughed more warmly now. "I never said it was completely unwanted... That's why we're having this conversation, after all."

Dalton's face brightened. "Only if you're sure."

"I am."

"In that case, I would love to kiss you."

Antoni flushed. "I'd like that."

He put his drink down and got to his feet. Dalton followed, coming closer. "Am I okay to put my arms around you? It won't hurt you, will it?"

"I'm fully healed, remember?"

Dalton stepped in front of him. He was an inch or so shorter than Antoni—nothing to cause problems. He put his hands lightly on Antoni's waist. "Is that okay?" he whispered.

Antoni answered with his lips, leaning forward to press them against Dalton's. Dalton moved his hands around Antoni's back, holding him. It didn't feel weird, or frightening, or uncomfortable. It felt great. Antoni wrapped his arms around Dalton, discovering the strong frame beneath his clothes. It was only now, when embracing another man, that he realised how skinny his own body had become.

Dalton murmured and pressed his tongue into Antoni's mouth.

His head swirled. The sensation of kissing this sexy, cheery guy after so many months of misery was overpowering. Dalton must have felt the force of his heartbeat against his chest.

"Still okay?" Dalton asked, pressing his forehead against Antoni's, cupping a hand against the back of his head.

"Perfect," he replied, breathing rapidly.

"We can take things slowly," Dalton assured him. "You set the pace."

Antoni hugged him a little tighter. "This is good for now."

"It sure is." Dalton stroked the curve of his spine.

After a moment, Antoni said, "I don't think I can go all the way...not tonight."

"That's okay," Dalton murmured, fluttering his lips across Antoni's jaw. "We don't have to."

"I mean, I'd like to, but it's been so long... I don't even have any condoms or lube in the house."

They both laughed.

"I didn't come to Nyemouth looking for sex, so I don't have any, either," Dalton said. "There are other things we can do. Lots of them."

Relief surged through him. Though the condom excuse was true, Antoni found the experience of being with Dalton a little overwhelming. He hadn't had sex in over a year. He wasn't ready to jump right to the full experience on their first night together.

They kissed again. His body was willing. The strong erection he pushed against Dalton was evidence of that.

Antoni had been worried following his surgery that things might not return to normal afterwards—that he might never have sex the way he was used to again. The doctor had assured him his body would make a full recovery, and there was no reason why he couldn't enjoy a fulfilling sex life.

When he'd met Dalton last night, he'd had no idea he would be the man to guide him on those first steps back to normality. He didn't even know he was ready to consider it.

One step at a time, he reminded himself.

Standing there, holding and kissing Dalton, was a massive step forward. And forward was the only way he wanted to go.

At last, he broke the embrace.

"Are you still okay?" Dalton asked.

Without another word, Antoni took his hand and led him to the bedroom.

Chapter Eleven

It was an extraordinary and strangely helpless feeling. This was Antoni's own home, and he may as well have been a stranger as he turned on the bedside lamp and closed the curtains. He was conscious of every move, every step he made. Dalton hovered in the doorway, watching, as though waiting for permission to enter.

"Come in," Antoni told him, surprised by the courage in his own voice. Brave was the last thing he felt right now.

"It's another lovely room," Dalton said, coming towards him. "Did you design it yourself?"

"I wouldn't call it 'designed'. I chose the carpet and the wallpaper. The rest I picked up on my ramblings. It's all pre-owned, rescued stuff."

"You have a great eye. It must be the photographic instinct in you. You could have a fantastic second career as an interior decorator whenever the mood suited you. People would pay a fortune to have a bedroom like this."

Like all compliments, Antoni laughed it off. It was flattering to hear it said aloud and to know Dalton liked his flat as much as he did. It had been so hard to find comfort of any kind these last six months, but now he was living back here rather than in Roger's spare room, it was a return to normalcy. In a strange way, it was important to him that Dalton should approve.

Why? Antoni didn't know yet, but it just was.

Dalton stepped in front of him. His eyes were large and dark in the warm glow of lamplight. He looked younger, more innocent. He put a hand on Antoni's shoulder and came in for another kiss. Soon their mouths were open, yielding against each other as they pushed their tongues together.

Dalton pulled back and murmured, "You taste so good."

Antoni put his hands on Dalton's waist, then, feeling brave, he slipped lower, copping a feel of his meaty arse. Sparks of desire ignited as he realised just how long it had been since he'd held a man. *Too long.* There was no ignoring the effect he had on Dalton, either. The hard bulge in his trousers was obvious.

Dalton buried his face in Antoni's neck, pressing his lips to his skin. Antoni shuddered, and Dalton moved his hands to his belt buckle.

"Is this okay?" he asked.

Antoni nodded.

"Stop me if it becomes too much for you."

Antoni was grateful for his consideration and sensitivity, but now he had started to heat up, he realised he could go further than he had anticipated. He pushed his hips against Dalton's hand to confirm his willingness.

Dalton grazed his tongue along Antoni's neck, causing him to shudder uncontrollably while he unbuckled his belt. He unfastened Antoni's jeans and shucked them over his thighs, before sliding down his body and exploring his torso with hands and lips until his face drew level with his groin. Dalton nuzzled the hard outline of his cock through his underwear. Antoni jerked at the unfamiliar contact.

"Oh my God." He took deep breaths. Dalton stared up at him. His eyes were wide, seeking assurance. "Don't stop. *Please*, don't stop."

With a slight, sexy curl of the lip, Dalton got back to work. He ran his mouth all along the shaft of Antoni's cock, mouthing him through his pants. Antoni watched in blissful wonder and ran his fingers over Dalton's head, pushing into the softness of his hair.

"You have a great cock," Dalton said.

"You haven't even seen it yet."

"We can fix that right now." He hooked his fingers into the waist of Antoni's underpants and slipped them down.

Antoni knew he had a good-sized penis, but it didn't stop a stab of self-consciousness as he was exposed. Dalton murmured appreciatively as he tugged Antoni's underwear to just above his knees.

"Yeah. I was right. That's a great cock." He cupped his hands around Antoni's balls, exerting just enough pressure to make him throb even harder. Then he swept his tongue along the underside of his cock, going smoothly from the base to the sensitive tip.

"Is it okay to pull back your foreskin?" Dalton asked.

"Uh-huh," Antoni replied and nodded.

Dalton took hold just beneath the head. "I know not all guys are comfortable with this."

"I'm good," Antoni answered. "More than good."

Dalton carefully slipped his foreskin back to reveal the dark pink head beneath. His breath was a warm rush against the sensitive organ. He opened his mouth and took it into the hot, wet interior. Antoni's legs weakened, and he had to put both of his hands on Dalton's shoulders to steady himself. He widened his stance as far as his clothing would allow.

Dalton worked slowly, using his mouth and hands, applying a light amount of pressure — just enough to feel utterly amazing. He moved his head back and forth, so wet and smooth, and took Antoni from nought to sixty in a few moments.

"Oh, God," Antoni exclaimed. A rush ran all through his body. "You'll have to stop... I can't last."

"I think you need this. I need it, too," Dalton said before taking him inside again.

Antoni's knees buckled, and he gripped Dalton's shoulders more tightly. The spasms started inside, in his prostate, then they pulsed right through him, intensifying in his balls. It was like the most pleasurable electric current had been run through his lower region. Dalton's mouth took him to the peak of orgasm and held him there, a prisoner for an aching age, before his body surrendered and released his load into Dalton's apparently eager throat.

Antoni cried to the ceiling, gasping with delight and ecstasy. Dalton kept him in his mouth until his trembling thighs were still, then sank back onto his haunches with a grin.

"Good?" he asked.

"The best. But I'm sorry. I didn't want to come so soon."

"The night is young," Dalton told him. "I'd like to make you come a lot more than that if you'll let me."

Antoni glowed with delight. Dalton was just too cute...too sexy. And he had a wicked sense of humour. Antoni had often wondered what would happen when he eventually hooked up with a guy after so long. Now, he didn't have to wonder. Dalton was the perfect partner. There was no awkwardness or embarrassment with him, just hot fun.

"Let's get naked."

Antoni shed his own clothes while watching with interest as Dalton undressed. He must have spent a lot of time keeping in shape. His upper body was strong, with well-shaped chest and shoulder muscles. His flat abdomen was hidden beneath a layer of dark hair.

"You go to the gym a lot?"

Dalton gave a self-depreciating shrug. "A couple of times a week, only for an hour at most. It's mainly a health thing. I'm not interested in bulking up like a lot of guys. I jog a least once a week, too. That's enough."

Antoni couldn't stop comparing his own torso to Dalton's. He was so skinny and shapeless in comparison to him. A lack of appetite and all his nervous energy had prevented him from regaining the weight he'd lost post-surgery. Self-consciously, he rubbed his fingers along the wide scar that tracked from just below his ribcage, all the way around his back.

Dalton noticed the gesture. "Does it still hurt?"

"No. It's fully healed. It can sometimes be stiff when I stretch, but that's all. It's as good as new."

Dalton lowered his gaze, as though sensing Anton's discomfort at being observed, and continued undressing. Antoni admired his chunky thighs as he tugged off his trousers. He loved how strong and hairy they were. When Dalton stood straight in just his black boxer-briefs, the strength of his arousal was obvious.

"Want to see more?" he asked cheekily.

"I'm already naked," Antoni replied. "It's only fair."

"I'm all about fairness." Dalton slipped his briefs to his ankles in one fluid effort and kicked them aside.

Antoni took a quick breath.

Dalton's cock jutted forward, thick and veiny with a long foreskin. His pubic hair was trimmed to a tidy bush, and his balls were smooth. Everything was perfect.

Antoni perched on the edge of the bed, taking in the view. Dalton seemed completely unabashed by his nudity and gave his balls a gentle tug as he stood for inspection.

Antoni raised a hand, beckoning him. Dalton loped across the room and tumbled on top of him. His weight was a sudden and unexpected delight. Laughing, they shuffled their way up the bed, entwinning their limbs and brushing their cocks together. The heat of skin against skin, the pressure of another body on top of him was incredible. Antoni realised in an urgent rush what he'd been missing.

Dalton pushed onto his elbows, easing the pressure. His face, just inches above Antoni, was more handsome than ever. He ran his fingertip across Antoni's jaw, stroking his lips.

"My God, you're stunning," Dalton whispered, closing the statement with a kiss.

Antoni stretched languorously beneath him, pushing his hips against Dalton's to feel the moist hardness of his cock. There was a stickiness between them, and Antoni was already hard again. He wanted to make Dalton come.

With a little encouragement, Dalton climbed on top, straddling Antoni's torso.

"Let me know if I'm too heavy," he said. "I don't want to put pressure on your scar."

He loved that Dalton was so considerate. "I'm fine," Antoni assured him, and curled his hand around Dalton's cock. *Oh wow.* So thick and juicy. They were equally matched in length, but Dalton had more girth. Antoni put his other hand on Dalton's torso and gripped the firm flesh. His body was perfect.

Antoni jerked him slowly to begin, noting his reactions, getting a feel for what he did and didn't like. There was no single technique that suited all guys. The way he liked to tug himself might not work for others. Dalton responded to the pressure of his thumb on the triangular section beneath the head. He listened and responded to Dalton's rapturous moans, and Antoni soon felt the wet patter of pre-cum on his chest.

Dalton's thighs trembled. He dug his heels into Antoni's legs, gently rocking on top of him. He put both hands on either side of Antoni's ribcage, and his breath came in ragged gasps as he turned his head from side to side. He came in shuddering propulsions, shooting long ropes of cum that hit Antoni's neck and chin, splattering him with his hot load.

"Sorry," Dalton said afterwards, gasping for breath. "I had no idea I would come that hard."

Antoni laughed, maintaining a soft grip on his dick. Dalton's heavy buttocks rested on his own hard cock. "It's hot," he admitted, wiping some of the cum from his neck and sucking his fingers.

"Whoa," Dalton said. "You like that?" He scooped up some of the cum himself and fed it to Antoni, who licked his fingers appreciatively.

"I've forgotten half the things I like in bed," he said. "I'm learning fast this evening."

* * * *

Antoni slept soundly for the first time in months, not waking until after eight. Though they hadn't really fallen asleep until around three am, he woke refreshed and full of energy. Most nights, insomnia kept him awake, and he would often give up around five and get out of bed, but with Dalton sleeping soundly beside him, he was in no hurry to leap out from under the covers that morning.

They had stayed true to their word and had not gone all the way without condoms but had discovered so many ways to give each other pleasure. Antoni had come three times before falling asleep. He hadn't achieved numbers like that since he'd been a teenager.

Dalton's breathing was deep and even. He was far away from waking.

Antoni stretched, leaning against Dalton's naked body but taking care not to disturb him. The close contact of bare skin against skin was electrifying. He had denied the pleasure two bodies could give each other for too long. Even before the attack the past year, he had pushed people away. The breakdown of his relationship with Harry had been devastating. Until then, he had never experienced anything so painful, and he'd dealt with it by shutting down. He'd had no interest in another boyfriend, still clinging to the hope that Harry would change his mind and come back. Then later, after the attack and his surgery, he'd been afraid of strangers and hadn't wanted anyone he didn't know coming near him.

Just a few days ago, he would have said the same. He didn't want a relationship of any kind, least of all a sexual one.

Dalton Caine had changed all that in a day and a half.

Leaving Dalton to sleep on, Antoni slid out of bed. He tip-toed to his closet, took out a pair of lounge pants and a T-shirt and crept to the bathroom. Dalton had been through so much in the last day, too. The poor guy needed to rest.

Having relieved himself and put on the lounge wear, Antoni headed to the kitchen. He wanted to make breakfast for the two of them, but given Dalton was a vegetarian, his weekend staple of bacon or sausages was out. He checked the fridge and found a good supply of eggs, half a box of mushrooms and red and green peppers. It would have to be poached eggs or omelette. He would let Dalton decide once he woke up.

He put on the kettle for tea and located his phone, going straight to local news sites for any updates on Catherine. *Nothing.* The search had been called off, as they already knew, and there were no further developments. At least Dalton wouldn't wake up to a terrible surprise.

He seemed to have convinced himself that his sister's disappearance was a stunt, and she would turn up soon. Antoni prayed he was right. Given all he'd been through himself, he struggled to be so optimistic. He couldn't shake the feeling that the situation might not be as straightforward as Dalton hoped.

Antoni was sitting at the table, enjoying a cup of tea and listening to an easy Sunday morning radio show when Dalton came through. Dressed in his underpants and last night's top and with his hair in sleepy disarray, he was a sexy sight. Antoni got straight up and poured him a glass of orange juice.

"Sit," he said. "Let me make you breakfast."

Dalton slumped into the chair. "You don't have to feed me."

"I want to," Antoni said, pulling the box of eggs from the fridge. "How do you want this? I can do poached eggs, scrambled or an omelette?"

"It's too much trouble," he said, sipping the juice. "Toast and tea will be fine."

"I like to cook, remember? Now, what's the answer?" He wiggled the egg carton.

Dalton grinned in defeat. "Okay, if you insist. I love poached eggs…if it's not too much effort."

Antoni waved aside his protest and pulled his large pan from the cupboard. He filled it with water and set it on the hob to boil with a splash of vinegar.

"I didn't wake you, did I? You looked so peaceful. I didn't want to disturb you."

"No. I would usually be up by now, anyway. Most Sunday mornings, I go for a run first thing. I like the peace and quiet when everyone else is still in bed. And I like to get it out of the way so I can enjoy the rest of the day. Sunday is usually my only day off, though most weeks I'll have something to look over while I'm at home — paperwork, licenses, permits, that kind of thing. How about you?"

"I work most weekends, too. Not as many hours now that we have Ethan to help, but the gallery is open seven days a week."

"Are you working today?"

Antoni took the toaster from another cupboard and set it on the counter. "Yes, but not until later. Roger is going to open. I'll relieve him at one."

"You two have a great relationship — personally and professionally."

"We do." Antoni carved thick slices of white bread from the loaf he'd bought yesterday.

"You do realise this is now the second meal you've treated me to?"

He saw Dalton grinning at him from the corner of his eye. "I'm just being a good host. It's how my parents raised me."

Dalton got to his feet and crossed the kitchen. He swung his arms around Antoni from behind and nuzzled his chin into his neck. Antoni relaxed into his hold. *That feels great.*

"You must let me return the favour. I want to take you to dinner…tonight."

He flushed. He hadn't expected to get together again so soon. "Well, if you're free. We'll have to see if there's any news about Cath—"

Dalton tickled him around the waist. Antoni yelped and laughed but couldn't pull away.

"No excuses. Tonight, okay? I'll call that place you told me about. The Lobster Pot, right? That's your favourite?"

Antoni started to protest. "It's too expensive." Dalton tickled him again.

"I said no excuses. I'll book a table for seven-thirty, okay? Make sure you bring a good appetite, because I want you to have all your favourites."

There was no point in arguing. Antoni had already realised that he found Dalton impossible to resist.

Chapter Twelve

Dalton returned to the hotel for a quick shower and a change of clothes. Despite the concern caused by his sister's disappearance, he couldn't stop grinning as he went about his business. Antoni had brightened his mood in a way that didn't seem possible, given the current circumstances. Dalton would have happily cancelled the rest of the day and spent it with Antoni, but that wouldn't be fair. Antoni had to work at the gallery. Besides, they had agreed to see each other again that evening, so he didn't have long to wait.

Just a few more hours. Time would drag, but Dalton was sure he could manage, especially for the reward he would receive at the end of it.

Once dressed, he called Justin for an update, but when he didn't answer his phone, Dalton decided to go straight around to the house.

Catherine's boyfriend answered the door in a pair of boxers and a creased T-shirt. He looked like he had slept in them. His hair stuck up at crazed angles, and his eyes were tight slits. He screwed up his face against the morning light as he tried to focus on Dalton.

"Any news?" Dalton asked.

Justin shook his head. The stale smell of alcohol wafted off him.

"Can I come in for a minute?" he asked when Justin didn't offer.

Justin nodded, rubbed his eyes and turned away. Dalton closed the door and followed him along the hall, which was littered with empty glasses and plates. Justin tugged his shorts out of his arse crack as he walked unsteadily to the kitchen.

Through the open door to the dining room, Dalton saw the debris of Friday's night's party—more empty glasses, wine bottles, plates of food, napkins. The kitchen was even worse, with empties cluttering every surface. The sweet and sour smell of food turning bad permeated the place.

"Did no one clear up?" he asked.

Justin hitched onto a stool at the breakfast bar, where a laptop stood open. "I didn't have time. The cleaner doesn't come at the weekend. It will get sorted tomorrow."

Plates of half-eaten food were piled up beside the sink. Justin seemed oblivious to it all and tapped away at his keyboard.

Dalton cranked open a window to let fresh air in and opened the cupboard doors, starting with the ones beneath the sink until he located a roll of rubbish bags. He tore one off and started tipping the wasted food inside.

"Just leave it," Justin said distractedly. "It'll get done tomorrow."

"And what if Catherine comes home before then? Today," he said. "She'll go berserk if she walks into this mess. Let me clear away the waste before it really goes off."

Justin shrugged without taking his eyes off the screen.

"Have you spoken to the police this morning?" Dalton asked, filling the first bag. The stench of seafood that had been left out for two nights almost made him heave. He focused on breathing through his mouth.

"I rang them when I got up. They said they would call later with an update. They don't give a shit. When a grown woman goes missing, it's low on their list of priorities."

Given Catherine's history, it was no surprise, but after the reaction he'd got at Catherine's flat from Justin and her friend Larissa, Dalton didn't mention it. Instead, he said, "I'm sure they mean it. They'll let you know as soon as they find anything."

Justin finally looked up from the computer screen. His eyes were more focused. "You're convinced she's fine, aren't you? That nothing bad has happened to her."

Dalton continued with the job of cleaning. "I don't think she's *fine*. No. That's not what I said. Catherine has mental health issues that have never been fully resolved, not enough to seriously hurt herself. I'm certain of that. But this is consistent with her previous behaviour. I think she's taken herself off somewhere — for whatever reason, I couldn't even guess at — but she'll come back in another day or two, just like she always does. And maybe this time, she'll get the help she needs to address whatever is triggering her."

He was aware of Justin's eyes boring into him. Dalton stacked the cleared plates in the sink and turned to face him. For a moment, neither of them spoke.

"Do you want to know what triggers her?" Justin said at last.

"If it will help us find her, of course I do."

Justin gestured to his laptop screen. "Have you looked at her social media accounts?"

"Briefly," he admitted, "but I'm not into that stuff. I don't follow it in any detail. Why? Has she posted something that hints at where she might be?"

Justin sucked his teeth. "No, nothing like that. She hasn't posted anything since Friday night. That isn't what I'm getting at. Catherine's an influencer. She has hundreds of thousands of followers who love what she posts and react positively to it. But it's not all good. If you followed her and read the comments some people post on her photos, you would know that."

"Trolls, you mean?"

Justin nodded.

"Does she take notice of that kind of thing?"

"It would take a thick-skinned individual not to. Catherine puts on a brave front, but she's sensitive underneath." Justin turned back to the screen. "These are some of the comments on the pictures she posted on Friday from the party. *Fake bitch. OMG, you really think you're hot. Lol, so ugly. The size of that chin. Are you a man?*" He continued scrolling through the comments. "*Ugly bitch. Fat cow. Waste of oxygen. Where are your tits?*"

Dalton winced. "Some people have nothing better to do. It's petty. Does Catherine pay attention to that rubbish?"

Justin continued, "*Just die already. Do us all a favour and fuck right off. The world would be a far better place without parasitic trash like you. Please kill yourself.*"

Dalton was appalled. "Seriously? People have actually written *that*? In a public place, for anyone to read?"

"This is all from one photo on Friday. She gets this shit all the time. I'm picking out the worst. There are a lot of complimentary messages, too, but a fuck-load of people hate her for being so popular. And these are only the public comments. She gets sent a lot of private messages along similar lines."

"It's disgusting," Dalton said, leaning over Justin's shoulders to read them for himself.

"*Now*, do you understand why I'm worried?"

"Does she take this stuff to heart?"

"Of course she does. There could be a hundred positive comments, and Catherine will focus on the one telling her how ugly she is. Despite what you seem to think, she is human, you know?"

"But it's just inadequate people venting their own self-loathing."

"That's not the way she sees it."

Dalton's eyes were drawn to one particular message.

Why don't you do the world a favour and kill yourself?

"Fucking hell."

For the first time he experienced a pang of genuine concern. *Is Catherine so fragile that she would take this toxic shit to heart? Worse still, is she damaged enough by the constant attacks to act upon them?*

* * * *

With forty-five minutes to spare until he was due to take over from Roger at the gallery, Antoni crossed the bridge to the north side of the river. He was in the mood for fresh air and a light lunch, nothing that would sit too heavy while he worked that afternoon. He decided to get something from one of the fish stalls that lined the side of the marina. It was early in the year, and they wouldn't have a full range to choose from, but a couple of the stalls still opened on Sunday to take advantage of the casual day visitors who came to walk their dogs along the beach.

Antoni's steps were light as he strolled along the waterfront. It was amazing just how good he felt. One night with Dalton had brightened his mood in a way he wouldn't have thought possible just a few days earlier. He hadn't believed he was ready for a physical relationship of any kind — not now, and maybe not for a long time. Fate had other ideas. Meeting the right man at the right time had changed everything for the better.

He couldn't resist glancing at Dalton's hotel as he walked by. Dalton had said he had a room overlooking the harbour. Looking up at the windows of Quay House, he wondered which one was his. Was he behind one of them right now?

Antoni inhaled deeply, calming the giddiness in his stomach.

He had to slow this down. There was a risk his emotions would get ahead of him. They had only known each other a couple of days, and Dalton would be leaving in a few more. Antoni couldn't afford to get too involved.

Why the hell not?

Life was short. His recent experiences had taught him how soon it could be over. Should he really hold back now?

He would see Dalton again this evening. Best to let things develop between them and without expectations or barriers in place. He owed himself that much.

As he walked along the harbour, he was delighted to see a familiar figure working on the deck of his boat below.

Harry Renner, Antoni's ex-boyfriend and fellow survivor of last year's horrific attack on South Pier... Harry had recently taken delivery of his new boat and had re-named it *Absent Friends*. He seemed to spend every spare minute preparing the vessel for the start of the tourist season.

"Hey," Antoni called down. "Do you ever take a break?"

Harry looked up, shielding his eyes from the sun with his hand, and grinned. "Hey, how are you doing?"

"Just going to get something to eat before I take over at the gallery."

Harry glanced at his watch. "I didn't realise the time. Mind if I join you? I had breakfast at seven and nothing since."

Harry effortlessly climbed the ladder from the deck of his boat to the dock.

"Is Christian not around?" Antoni asked.

"He's working on his book. I thought I'd leave him in peace. I've got plenty to do on the boat. We've arranged to go for a late lunch around four, but I'll never last that long."

"How is he?" Like Antoni, Christian had suffered serious abdominal injuries that had required surgery in the incident last year.

"He's okay. Pretty good, all things considered. He still has a few minor issues, but nothing he can't handle." Harry paused, giving Antoni a quick glance over. "Hey, you're looking well."

He grinned. "I feel it."

Harry patted his shoulder. "I'm glad to hear it. I can't put my finger on what it is, but there's something different about you, almost like a new person. Still too thin, though. Let's get something to eat and fill you up."

They walked along the side of the harbour towards the food stalls.

When they had first separated, Antoni had taken the breakup hard. Though he could look back and see their relationship had been coasting for several years, at the time, he couldn't accept it. Even last autumn, when Harry had first got together with Christian, Antoni had still tried to win him back. He knew it wouldn't have worked. There was nothing like a near-death experience to bring clarity. He was glad to see Harry and Christian so happy together. His own relationship with Harry was stronger, too. Without the romantic attachment, they were the best of friends.

As they approached the food stalls, he caught Harry watching him from the side. As Harry furrowed his brow in curiosity, Antoni couldn't contain his smile.

"What are you not telling me?" Harry asked, matching his grin. "Something has happened, hasn't it? I haven't seen you this happy in years. What is it? Did you win the lottery?"

"I wish. But no, it's nothing like that." In many ways it was better. Through a night with Dalton, he had won a part of himself back.

"So, what is it? You're not grinning like the Cheshire Cat for nothing."

Antoni ignored him and approached the fish stall. They had the usual display of prawns, mussels, cockles and crayfish, as well as dressed crab, lobster and fresh oysters. He didn't want to spoil his appetite for the evening, so he chose a large pot of prawns with a generous slice of lemon on top. Harry went with his usual order, three oysters with lemon juice, and they retired to a bench overlooking the harbour to enjoy them.

It was a bright enough afternoon, though there was a noticeable chill off the water, and Antoni was glad he had worn a jacket.

"As nice as I know those prawns are, I don't believe they're the cause of your goofy smile," Harry said. "So come on. Spill the beans. Tell me what's made you so happy?"

"Am I usually so miserable?" Antoni joked.

"I wouldn't say 'miserable'. No, that's a bit harsh. But you've never had the sunniest disposition," Harry said, nudging Antoni with his elbow to show he was jesting. "Whatever it is, I'm happy for you. It's nice to see you in such a grand mood."

Antoni chewed one of the prawns slowly, weighing up whether to say something or not. *What the hell.* He swallowed. "I met someone on Friday night. I hardly know him, really, but from the little time we've spent together, I like him."

"Aw. That's brilliant. It's about time, too."

"Don't get too excited. I'm trying not to. He's not from around here. He's only visiting, but we went out last night, and we've got another date this evening."

"Don't let the fact he's visiting put you off. Christian was only here on a two-week holiday when we met, too. I had a few reservations about that, but I'm glad I ignored them. You should, too." Harry brought a shell to his lips, tipped back his head and slid the oyster into his mouth. He chewed gently before swallowing. "How long is he here for?"

"That's the thing, I don't know. Did you hear about the woman who went missing yesterday? The one they launched the lifeboat for? Well, that's his sister. I think he was originally planning to leave yesterday, but he's going to stick around until there's some news."

Harry winced. "Shit. Hardly the greatest circumstances to begin a relationship. Still, things weren't much better for Christian and me in that department, either. It worked out well in the end."

"I don't want to put those expectations on us," Antoni said. "It is what it is for now. We'll see what, if anything, happens next."

"Come on then, tell me. Does this guy have a name?"

"Dalton." Antoni explained how they had met at Catherine's party and the way things had developed from there. Harry was clueless when it came to social media and had no idea who Catherine was, other than having heard about her bar. "Christian was keen to check it out one time, but we've heard nothing but bad reports about it. We've given it a miss so far."

"It's nothing special," Antoni remarked, and immediately felt a pang of guilt for bad-mouthing it. "The funny thing is, Dalton doesn't believe anything serious has happened to her." He gave Harry a potted version of their family history and Catherine's previous disappearances.

"Well, he's her brother and he doesn't sound worried, so maybe there's nothing to it. It's pretty shitty if it is a hoax—not just for the family but for the lifeboat. That search yesterday will have run to thousands."

"You know it doesn't work like that. If there's a chance, however slim, that she did go into the sea, they had to look for her."

"I know. But if it all turns out to be a sick stunt, she should be ashamed of herself."

Antoni sighed. "I don't know her well enough to make that judgement. Thankfully, Dalton seems a lot more grounded and honest than his sister."

"I'm glad to hear it. You deserve a bit of happiness with a decent fellow."

Antoni laughed. Harry was getting ahead of himself, but it was difficult not to share his enthusiasm. He found it hard not to get carried away with his thoughts and feelings for Dalton, too.

One step at a time, he reminded himself.

But it was impossible to keep a lid on how happy these few days together had made him. He was dying to see Dalton again.

Their date at the restaurant could not come soon enough.

Chapter Thirteen

Dalton spent over three hours at Justin's house, clearing the worst of the mess from Friday's party. He loaded and ran the dishwasher four times, bagged up all the food waste and empty bottles and put them out for collection. He spotted a group of rats in the garden making the most of the leftovers out there. He wasn't about to deal with that problem and kept the doors shut. Justin's cleaners could have the pleasure of the outdoor mess.

Justin only left his laptop to get a can of Coke from the fridge. While Dalton worked on debris, Justin read aloud the worst of the comments posted on Catherine's social media pages.

Dalton did his best to get him away from it. He tried to encourage Justin to help him tidy the house for Catherine's return, but he wouldn't be swayed. All he wanted to do was trawl through her posts, wallowing in the dregs of what those anonymous internet warriors had to say.

By the time he'd sorted the bulk of the mess, Dalton had had enough. There was still plenty to do. All the surfaces needed a thorough wash and the carpets needed to be vacuumed, but he wasn't about to offer.

"You should think about taking a shower and getting dressed," he told Justin when he was finished. "It's almost two."

Justin finally tore his eyes away from the screen. "Huh?" He looked at his watch. "Oh, shit. Yeah. Right."

"And eat something. There's a freezer full of leftovers. You have plenty to choose from."

He got up from his chair, stretched and scratched his belly. He looked around, seeming to notice the difference Dalton had made to the place. "You didn't have to do all this."

"I couldn't leave it." Dalton put his hand on Justin's shoulder. "Have a bite to eat and get dressed, okay? You'll feel much better. And I know you don't believe me, but Catherine could walk through that door at any minute. You don't want her to find you like this, do you?"

"I suppose not."

"Good. Now, look after yourself. I'll call you later for an update, but you have my number if anything happens in the meantime. Right?"

He nodded. "I will. And thanks."

When Dalton returned to the hotel, he realised he was hungry himself. They were still serving food in the main bar, so he ordered a bowl of soup and a bread roll to see him through until his dinner with Antoni. As he waited for the food to arrive, he realised that he hadn't actually booked the table for that evening. He didn't have the number, so as soon as he finished eating, he walked over to The Lobster Pot.

The restaurant was coming to the end of their lunch service, and there were still a lot of occupied tables. He went straight to the bar where a handsome waiter with thick black hair and dark eyes was wiping down the counter.

"Hey," Dalton said. "I know it's short notice, but is it possible to get a table for two for this evening?"

The waiter dried his hands on a towel. "I imagine so. We've got a few bookings, but I don't think we're full." He guided Dalton to the front desk and tapped at the keys of a laptop. "What time did you have in mind?"

"Around seven-thirty."

The man nodded. "That's fine. Can I take a name and number?"

"Dalton Caine," he answered, and reeled off his phone number.

The man's fingers paused over the keyboard, and he looked at Dalton, his brow furrowing. "Caine? Are you any relation to Catherine Caine?"

"I'm her brother," he said. "Do you know Catherine?"

The man gave a short snort through his nostrils, and Dalton noticed a stiffening of his posture. "I know her. We went out together for a few months last year." An unmistakable hardness had crept into his voice.

"Oh, right. I wasn't aware. This is my first visit. I take it you've heard the news? That she's missing."

He nodded and sighed. "Yes…and I'm sorry. It must be a worry for you. I should have said that in the first place." He extended his hand. "My name is Paul…Paul Madden."

Paul was seemingly in his early forties and as different from Justin as it was possible to be. With his dark good looks, thick head of hair and muscular physique, most people would consider him far more physically attractive than Catherine's current man. The other, most obvious difference between them was that Justin was a multi-millionaire and Paul was a waiter. Was his sister really that mercenary?

Dalton knew the answer. *Yes.*

"So..." Paul suddenly seemed awkward, a little embarrassed. "Have they, er...found her yet?"

"Nothing so far. How well did you know my sister?"

"Like I said, we went out for a few months. I used to work for her at the White Lady. She sacked me when we split up."

No surprise. "I'm sorry."

Paul shrugged his shoulders. "It wasn't the best place to work."

"I've heard."

"I prefer it here."

Dalton didn't know what else to say, but he felt that he had to say something. He knew so little about his sister's life in Nyemouth, and what he had heard so far gave a warped impression of her. "Can you spare a few minutes? I'd really like to talk to you about her."

Paul stiffened again. "I don't think I'm the best person to talk to about Catherine. We didn't..." He stumbled for words, licked his lips and swallowed. "Well, we didn't have the healthiest relationship, and our breakup got kind of nasty."

"Don't worry. I don't need you to sugarcoat it. I know exactly what she can be like. It's just, well, you knew her. You know more about her life than I do. It would mean a lot if you could help me to build a picture of what it's like for her. It might give me an idea of where to find her."

Paul hesitated. He cast his eyes around the restaurant and back to the bar, before looking at his watch. "Okay. We're in a bit of a lull just now. I can spare ten minutes, if you think it will help."

"Thank you. I really do."

He gestured to a seating area in the window. "Wait for me over there. I'll just let them know I'm taking a break. Can I get you a coffee or anything?"

"That would be great, thanks. White with one sugar, if it's not too much trouble."

Paul nodded and looked at him uncertainly one more time before going to speak to one of his colleagues. Dalton gazed out of the window while he waited. He didn't want to make Paul any more uncomfortable by watching him. He already looked tense enough.

It had been a fair morning and afternoon, but dark grey clouds were moving in from the northwest. He hoped the weather would hold for his date with Antoni later, though neither of them had far to walk if it took a turn for the worse. Dalton could even see the window of his hotel from here. Unless he ventured up onto the cliffs, the town was compact and close together. He reckoned he could walk from the tip of the north pier, along the waterfront, across the bridge and down the other side to the south pier in around fifteen minutes — twenty, maximum.

Paul returned, carrying two oversized coffee cups and saucers on a tray with sugar and milk.

"I thought it best if you added what you want for yourself," Paul said, setting a cup down in front of him.

Dalton noticed Paul's broad shoulders and trim waist as he took the seat opposite. Looks weren't everything, he appreciated that, but Paul seemed much more suited to Catherine and her social media obsession than Justin. He imagined her posting dozens of envy-inspiring photos of them as a couple, in a way she didn't do with Justin.

Then again, maybe she didn't have the chance to. Catherine could be difficult to live with. Maybe Paul got tired of her demands and expectations.

Paul took his coffee black and unsweetened. He lifted the cup to his lips with two hands and blew on the surface before taking a sip.

He's still uncomfortable.

"I appreciate your time," Dalton said, hoping to relax him. "This is my first time in Nyemouth. I got here on Friday and Catherine disappeared on Saturday, so I'm still trying to put some of the pieces together — to get an idea of her life here."

After a moment, Paul nodded, seeming to accept the suggestion. "I'm not sure what I can tell you. We didn't end on the best of terms." He laughed. "Quite the opposite. It was a mess."

"Who finished the relationship?"

He chewed his lip, seeming to consider his answer. After a sigh, he said, "I did. Catherine had started seeing that other guy, Justin, but she thought we could continue as we were. We weren't living together or anything, so there were no commitments, and I didn't even know about Justin at first. I think she might have been going out with him for five or six weeks when I found out."

None of this came as a surprise. "I'm sorry. That can't have been easy."

Paul raised a weary smile. "Don't apologise. It's hardly your fault."

"Still... It's a shitty way to treat people."

Paul nodded. "I can't say I blame her. She treated me like a doormat from the start. Every part of our relationship was on her terms — when we saw each other, whether I stayed over or not. There were never any favours at work. She treated me as badly as the rest of the staff. And, like a mug, I took it. She probably thought she could keep me around as a bit on the side and I'd go along with it, like I'd gone along with everything else."

Dalton believed what he was hearing. There was no spite or anger in Paul's tone, just a shade of sadness and inevitability. "How did she take it? When you dumped her?"

Paul ran his finger around the rim of his coffee cup. "To say badly would be an understatement. Look... I don't know how much you want to hear. She's your sister, after all."

Dalton put both hands on the table and leaned forward. "I want to know it all. I've had my own difficulties with Catherine. I'm her younger brother, and it's no exaggeration to say she's been a pain in the arse for most of my life. I've experienced her wrath, like everyone else."

Paul didn't speak. He just looked at Dalton, breathing heavily through his nose.

He's going to cut this short.

"Please," Dalton urged.

At last Paul said, "I wonder how much you really know her."

"After thirty-one years, barely at all. That's why I'm here, trying to find out as much as I can."

"All right," Paul replied. "If you really want to know." He sat back in the chair and unbuttoned his shirt to just above the navel, before pulling it open to reveal his chest. His pecs were covered in dark brown hair, except for a large patch on the left side, more or less above his heart. It was six or seven inches long and approximately four or five inches across, triangular in shape. The flesh where the hair did not grow was pink and mottled.

It took a few seconds for Dalton's brain to comprehend what he was seeing. "Oh my God." His hand flew to his mouth, trembling. His eyes were already tearing up when he met Paul's gaze. "She did that to you?"

Paul allowed him to look at the damage for a few more moments before fastening his shirt back up. "That was a hot iron. I was asleep in my own flat. I didn't even know she had a key. She came in the middle of the night, turned on the iron, and when it was hot, she made her mark."

Dalton struggled to take it in. He knew his sister was twisted but had no idea she was that bad. "Fuck... Why isn't she in prison? Did you report this to the police?"

Paul shook his head. "No. She mocked me and said no one would believe it. She would tell them I was the one pissed off at her for leaving me and had done it to myself to get back at her."

"No one would believe that crap."

He shrugged. "Maybe not. She convinced me, just the same." He took another sip of coffee and patted his chest. "This might be the worst of it, but it wasn't the only thing she did to me when we were together..." He faltered and looked away, gazing out of the window.

"It's not too late to make a complaint."

Paul kept his focus outside. "She's missing. It won't do any good now."

"I think she'll be back," Dalton said.

He shrugged. "I hope not. Don't take it the wrong way, but I don't ever want to see her again." He turned to look at him. "Your sister is fucked up. She's dangerous. She could kill someone. I'm sure of it. I saw it in her eyes that night. I don't know what stopped her from killing me, but for a split second, I saw it cross her mind. I hope she's been washed far out to sea and is never found. That way, she can't ever hurt anyone again."

Chapter Fourteen

It was the longest day. Time dragged as Antoni waited to see Dalton. As soon as he closed the gallery, he bounded upstairs to the flat. He laid out his clothes on the bed — navy chinos, a pale blue shirt with a light paisley print, his newest pair of underpants and dark socks. He ran a deep bath and soaked in the tub with a bottle of beer, listening to an LP of old 1970s and 80s tunes through the open door.

Ethan had checked all the local social media pages before he left and assured Antoni that there had been no new developments in the search for Catherine. If Roger had been missing for so long, Antoni would not have been going on a date tonight. He would have torn the town apart to find him, but Dalton didn't have any great concern about his sister's disappearance.

Antoni wondered whether he was experiencing a delayed reaction. The gravity of the situation might not have hit him yet.

Antoni dried off and got dressed.

It was raining heavily when it came time to leave. He grabbed his umbrella and made his way down the narrow back streets, where it was sheltered from the worst of the downpour, arriving at The Lobster Pot five minutes early. It was too rough a night to wait outside, so he went straight in.

Dalton was already sitting at the bar.

Antoni's heart surged at the sight of him.

"Have you been here long?" he asked as he approached.

"About ten minutes. I was ready for seven and couldn't see the point of hanging around my hotel room. I guess I was too excited."

"How are you?"

"Great. Even better for seeing you. You look wonderful."

Antoni smiled shyly. He was working on it, but compliments were still difficult to take.

Dalton looked sexy as fuck in an open-necked white shirt and a dark jacket.

Their table was ready. Though the restaurant was busy and Dalton had only made the reservation that afternoon, they were given a great spot in the window, overlooking the marina. Antoni had been here more times than he could remember, and he had never been as excited as he was right now.

"What's good?" Dalton asked, studying the leather-bound menu.

Antoni winced. "To be honest, I haven't tried any of the vegetarian dishes, so I can't recommend them. All the other food is first rate, so I have no doubt the veggie menu will be, too. We can go somewhere else if it's a struggle for you to choose."

"No way. This is your favourite, and I want to experience it with you. I'll find something on here to my liking."

Dalton settled on a starter of heirloom tomato and cucumber gazpacho with a main course of field mushroom burger with halloumi, grilled gherkins, beef-tomato salad, burger sauce and fries. He also ordered a side of green salad. Antoni had never seriously considered vegetarian food, but it did sound good. For himself, he overcame his reluctance to eat seafood in front of Dalton and chose a starter of prawn and smoked salmon cocktail followed by the house special shellfish platter, which included crab, mussels, prawns and half a lobster. He asked them to leave off the oysters.

Dalton requested a bottle of Veuve Clicquot champagne.

"Do you have something to celebrate? Good news?" Antoni asked when the waiter had left. Had there been a development that hadn't made the Nyemouth Facebook pages yet?

Dalton nodded. "I do." He leaned across the table, his voice lowered. "Being with you. If that's not a cause for champagne, I don't know what is. Do you?"

Antoni flushed. This man was almost too perfect. "I guess not."

Dalton asked how his work had gone.

"Nothing special," Antoni admitted. "Steady enough for this time of year, but we didn't sell much more than a few postcards and tea towels in the shop. The online orders kept me busy for a couple of hours. Things should pick up by the end of next month. How was your day?"

The waiter returned with the champagne, and they waited in silence, gazing happily across the table at each other while it was opened and poured. They raised their glasses and clinked.

"Cheers."

Dalton filled him in on the morning and his visit to see Justin. "It was a mess — and so was he."

"It sounds like he's struggling," Antoni said.

"I know, but it's kind of strange, don't you think? They haven't been together that long for him to fall apart like this."

"Everyone reacts to stress differently."

Dalton shook his head. "I don't know. There's something odd about it all, and I don't buy it." He sipped his drink. "Maybe Catherine has him totally enthralled, and he just can't live without her."

"Maybe."

"Or maybe he's as screwed up as she is."

"You're still not worried?"

Dalton was no longer smiling. "I keep changing my mind back and forth, but the longer this goes on, the more certain I am it's a game. Catherine loves to play with people, and judging by the state of Justin this morning, she's got him tied up in knots."

"Is she really that nasty?"

Dalton leaned over the table and lowered his voice even further. "You have no idea. Fuck, even I didn't know how bad she could be until today." His voice was a whisper. "I met one of her ex-boyfriends this afternoon. The poor guy has the scars to prove just how dangerous she is. I'm not talking about emotional scars, either, though I've no doubt she's left plenty of those behind, too. He has the *physical* scars she left on his body." He sighed and shook his head. "It's sickening.

She should have gone to jail for what she did to him. My sister is a monster."

Antoni reached out and put his hand on the back of Dalton's arm. "You can talk to me if it helps."

"I will…but not here. Catherine has ruined so much for so many people, but she's not going to spoil our date." He sat back and straightened. "Let's change the subject, eh? I've had more than enough of my sister for one day."

The first courses arrived, and they refreshed their glasses. The food was fantastic, and although Antoni wanted to respect Dalton's wish not to talk about Catherine, what he had just told him sparked fresh memories of the day he'd spent photographing her. Dalton was suggesting she had a power over people, an ability to hold them under her spell.

He wondered now whether there might be something in that.

When they had gone to the north beach for the photoshoot, Catherine had been accompanied by her friend, Larissa. They had an unusual relationship. Catherine offered her friend little encouragement, while giving her several bitchy put downs. When Antoni had suggested they might like a few pictures together, Catherine had ridiculed the idea.

"If she wants her own shots, she can get her own fucking photographer and pay for them. You're here to make me look good and nothing else."

He had forgotten that bizarre interaction until now. At the time, he'd wondered why Catherine had even brought her friend along if she wasn't going to participate. It seemed she wanted Larissa there for no other reason than to watch and adore her. The friendship was stacked on one side. That had been obvious. Larissa bore the brunt of Catherine's barbed remarks without a hint of comeback.

Was Larissa just one more person caught under her spell?

He found it hard to understand. From his point of view, Catherine lacked the charm, warmth and personality of her brother. Why were so many people enraptured by her?

When Dalton excused himself to use the bathroom between courses, Antoni pulled out his phone and logged into his cloud account to view the shots from that day on the beach. He scrolled through the solo pictures of Catherine until he found what he was looking for. In several of the original, uncropped images, Larissa was caught in the background. He zoomed in on her.

Yes, no doubt about it.

Larissa gazed at Catherine with complete adoration.

Were they more than friends? Lovers, perhaps? It seemed likely that Catherine would keep someone so obviously in love with her in her orbit, while handing out enough meagre scraps of affection to keep them hooked.

He put his phone away. For Dalton's sake, he wouldn't mention it…not tonight. He would show him the photos and share his impressions tomorrow.

When Dalton returned, they finished the bottle of champagne. "Shall we have another?" he asked.

"I couldn't take much more fizz," Antoni admitted, "but a bottle of white wine would go nicely with the food."

They opted for a French chardonnay, which arrived just as their main courses did.

It was a perfect meal.

"I've always loved it here," Antoni admitted, feeling more than a little tipsy.

"I can understand why. It's got a great atmosphere, as well as amazing food."

"Fresh seafood is not a big part of our Polish cuisine. In fact, it's not at all. I first came here for a meal when I was around fifteen. It was a large birthday for one of my parents' friends, and it was the first time I'd ever had fresh shellfish. I've adored it ever since. I still love our traditional Polish food, but this place has always been a treat for me."

Dalton rested his chin on his hands and looked at Antoni through his long eyelashes. "Thanks for sharing it with me. The last two days have been a whirlwind of chaos, but the time I spend with you is so calm and relaxing. I can't explain how much I appreciate it."

A warm rush went all the way through him. Antoni leaned closer. "I'm glad to hear that. I must admit to feeling something similar. The last six months have been tough, but you've helped me in a way I wouldn't have thought possible just a few days ago. This is my third night out in a row. You know, that's three times more than I've been out since I was attacked."

Dalton reached across the table and took his hand. "It sounds like we have both been good for each other."

"We have," he agreed.

They were too full to order dessert or coffee and took their time finishing the wine.

Antoni couldn't remember the last time he had felt this carefree. It couldn't last. He knew Dalton would leave in a few more days and it would be over, but that was not a concern for tonight. Right now, they made each other happy, and that was better than anything.

Antoni twirled the wine glass between his fingers. "You know last night I said I needed to take things very slowly? In the bedroom."

Dalton nodded, gently biting his bottom lip.

"Well, I'm ready to go a bit further," Antoni said, his voice low and husky. "Maybe all the way."

Dalton's smile spread across his face. "That is good news."

"And also, last night, we didn't have any condoms. I went to the store today, and that's no longer a problem."

Dalton beamed even more brightly. "Great minds think alike, because so did I."

Antoni laughed and excitement tingled all through his body. He would not have had the nerve to be so forward on Thursday, but as their time was limited, they couldn't afford to waste it. "Shall we go to your place or mine?"

Dalton grinned and pointed out the window. "I can see my bedroom from here. So, I guess my place is nearer."

He raised his hand and signalled for the bill.

Chapter Fifteen

When they left the restaurant, it was raining with such force that the water bounced from the pavement a foot in the air. Dalton grabbed Antoni's hand, and they raced across the bridge, dodging puddles and laughing all the way. They were like kids, free of any care and worry and were soaked when they reached the entrance to Quay House. They hurried up the stairs to the room rather than wait for the elevator. Dalton took the lead and was thrilled when Antoni made a playful grab for his bum.

"Sorry," Antoni said from behind. "That was just too good to resist."

Dalton flashed a look over his shoulder. "You'll get no resistance from me."

He opened the door to his room, and they tumbled inside.

Dalton turned and grabbed Antoni as soon as they entered, pushing his mouth against his. Their lips yielded and they thrust their tongues against one another. Rainwater dripped from their brows and over their faces. Neither of them seemed to care.

"I've been wanting to kiss you like that all night," Dalton gasped, pushing his fingers through Antoni's soaking hair.

Antoni rubbed his thumbs across the rivulets that ran down Dalton's brow, keeping his eyes clear. "So have I. All day, in fact. I've been wanting to kiss you since you left this morning."

Dalton pulled him in for another lingering exchange.

"We should get out of these wet clothes," he said at last.

Antoni grinned. His breath was hot and heavily against his face. "We should."

Dalton went into the bathroom and returned with two fresh towels. He rubbed one over his hair before drying the water that poured down his neck and beneath his shirt. He moved the chair from the desk and set it in front of the radiator. "Hang your things over here. They should dry soon enough."

He took off his own shirt and threw it on the bathroom floor before unfastening his trousers and shrugging them off. The rain hadn't managed to soak as far as his underwear, though his erection tented the front of them and had created a damp patch of its own.

Antoni removed his shirt and placed it over the back of the chair. He wobbled as he tried to take off his trousers, laughing as he grabbed the wall for support. "I think all the wine has gone to my head," he said.

His body was beautiful in the soft light of the room. His pale skin took on a golden hue.

Dalton hurried to the bathroom and retrieved the box of condoms and bottle of lube he had picked up that afternoon.

Antoni sat on the bottom of the bed when he returned. He looked excited and more than a little nervous.

"How about some music?" Dalton asked, setting the condoms and lube on the bedside table.

"Good idea."

He grabbed his phone and activated his Bluetooth travel speakers. "It can't compete with your vintage record collection, but it's a lot handier when travelling." He brought up the playlist he used for relaxing on Sunday mornings, a mixture of easy listening tunes and classic stuff from the 1960s and 70s. The smooth sound of Otis Redding came through the small but effective speakers.

Antoni smiled, seemingly pleased with the choice.

Dalton sat beside him on the bed. He put an arm around his shoulders, pulling him close and savouring the heat of his body.

"We can do as much or as little as you'd like," he said. "I know last night was a breakthrough, but I don't want to rush you." He pressed his lips against Antoni's neck and tasted his skin. Antoni shuddered.

"I didn't think I was ready. When we went to bed yesterday, I wasn't sure what I would be capable of. I'm still not, if I'm honest. My body... It's been through so much. I don't know how far I can go."

Dalton held him tighter and nuzzled his neck. "You mean fucking?"

Antoni nodded.

"You don't need to worry about that. I'm going to take it all. I want you to enjoy my body and do whatever you want to...whatever feels good."

Antoni turned to look at him. "We haven't really discussed it, have we? What our preferences are."

"Oh, that's easy enough." He drew his tongue towards Antoni's ear, savouring his reaction, the way his skin rippled with gooseflesh. "I'm completely versatile."

"You are?" Antoni sounded surprised.

"Sure. I mean, I've probably done more topping than bottoming, but that's mainly because of the kind of guys I've been with. I actually have no preference. I enjoy it both ways." He brushed his fingers over Antoni's hard nipples. "How about you?"

"I'm the same," he said breathlessly. "My ex, Harry, liked to top, so I was more of a bottom with him, but I used to like it either way. Since my surgery, I haven't even considered bottoming. I'm not sure that I could."

"You don't have to worry about that tonight." He trailed his hand down, across Antoni's flat stomach, towards his waist. He was fully aware of the way Antoni's cock jutted inside his underpants, but he held off touching it, wanting to prolong the anticipation. "You don't have to worry about a thing. You'll know when you're ready. I'm going to give you everything you need for now."

Antoni leaned closer, and they locked mouths again, falling backwards to lie on the bed. Dalton moved his hand to Antoni's waist and shuffled closer, so their bodies touched. The contact of hard cock against cock was electric. They moaned into each other.

Dalton was aware of how important this must be for Antoni. He wanted to make it perfect. He didn't want to do anything that would startle him or put him off. They lay together, kissing and touching, neither in a hurry to go further as they enjoyed the moment. Antoni pressed his leg against Dalton, and Dalton opened his thighs, letting Antoni slide between them. The sensation of bare skin against skin drove him crazy.

They had enjoyed each other in so many ways the previous night, but this was even better.

Antoni moved his hand around Dalton's back and slipped inside his underpants, clutching his arse. Dalton moaned even more enthusiastically and pushed against him in encouragement. "Take them off," Dalton moaned.

Antoni shoved Dalton's underpants over his bum. Dalton shuffled on top of him, releasing his hard cock, and shoved his pants low enough for him to slither out of them. He kicked them off the edge of the bed.

"Now, that's better," he said, writhing on top of Antoni, completely naked.

"For you, maybe," Antoni said, wiggling beneath him to shuck off his own underwear. "Now, we're even."

Dalton took the weight on his hands and knees until they were both completely bare before lying down on top of Antoni again. They moved their hips, grinding their cocks together. Their dicks were both moist, creating a delicious slickness between them. The kisses continued. Dalton shuddered as Antoni caressed the small of his back with his fingers, tracing the curve of his spine before taking his bum in both hands.

"Are you sure you're ready?" Antoni asked, brushing his lips against Dalton's.

"I was ready the moment I saw you. Let's do it."

Dalton rolled to the end of the bed and grabbed the provisions. He tore into the box of condoms and handed one to Antoni before getting to work with the lube. He poured it over his fingers before stuffing them into the crack of his arse. He wouldn't admit it to Antoni, but it had been a while, and Antoni's cock was fairly girthy. Despite his hunger, he would need a lot of lube to take that the way he wanted it.

Antoni lay against the pillows, smoothing the condom down the length of his dick, securing it around the base. Dalton poured lube over the head and watched him get a slick coating all the way along the shaft. He applied more lube to his own fingers and pushed them into his bum, preparing the way.

"I think I'm good to go." He grinned.

"I'll let you lead." Antoni held his cock at the root, angling it straight up towards the ceiling.

It was all the encouragement Dalton needed. He climbed onto Antoni again and crawled across his body until his hips were on top of Antoni's. He lowered himself until Antoni's cock slipped into his crack, and he guided the head to his opening.

"Okay, here we go." Maintaining eye contact, he sank lower, feeling the blunt entry of hard flesh invading his own supple hole. He exhaled long and slow. "Whooooa, that feels good."

"Everything okay?" Antoni's hands rested on his hips.

"Damn right."

Dalton dug his heels against Antoni's thighs and sank lower, lower, filling his passage until his buttocks rested on Antoni's balls. He took him all the way. His own cock jutted forward, rock hard. Antoni moved his hand towards it.

"Better not touch me," Dalton warned. "I'm so turned on I'll blow like a rocket." He put his hands on Antoni's ribcage, careful not to apply too much pressure, and rocked gently until his body got used to the hard dick inside him. Once he was good and relaxed, he worked up and down, rising slowly, just an inch or two to begin with.

"Oh, God," he sighed. He hadn't felt this good in a long time. Getting fucked was an unexpected pleasure, heightened further by the connection he had with this wonderful man.

Antoni returned his hands to his hips and Dalton rode him, getting more adventurous and active as he relaxed. The friction of Antoni's cock against his prostate was insanely good. Each stroke sent waves of pleasure flowing through his body. Dalton leaned forward to kiss him as he rode, wanting to deepen their union.

Their skin was slick with sweat. Dalton could taste it on Antoni's top lip and feel the dampness of it in his hair. Antoni groaned, leaning his hips upwards, pushing into him. After a while, they rolled over. With Antoni on top, Dalton raised his legs, wrapping them around Antoni's hips, opening his body to receive and take him deeper. Antoni kissed him all the time as he maintained a steady thrust, moving inside him with determination but controlling his urgency.

"This is incredible," Dalton sighed, loving every second, every bit of friction.

Antoni murmured agreement. Dalton knew Antoni had to be holding back. To have gone without sex for long would take all the strength he had to control his passion.

"Let go," Dalton urged. "Do whatever you want. There'll be time enough to take it slowly later. Do what you need to do right now."

Antoni nodded and increased the pace of his thrusts. It made things even more intense for Dalton. The pleasure was dizzying. Dalton gripped him tighter, imploring him to go harder, faster. Antoni buried his head on Dalton's shoulder, soaking him with sweat while speeding up to a jack-rabbit pace. His cries of passion became more urgent and desperate sounding.

Dalton held him tight as he came. Antoni's entire body shuddered. His heart pounded against Dalton's chest. His thrusts became a series of short, staccato jabs, before fading away.

"Oh, God," he gasped, allowing some of his weight to sag against Dalton.

Dalton held onto him, stroking the back of his damp head, allowing him all the time he needed to savour the moment. This was a large step forward in Antoni's recovery. Dalton understood the importance of it.

After several minutes, Antoni took the weight on his elbows and raised himself above Dalton.

"Are you okay?" he asked, looking deep into his eyes.

"I'm perfect," Dalton answered truthfully.

"You didn't come."

"It doesn't matter. We've got plenty of time for that. You got back on the horse. Isn't that what matters?"

Antoni crinkled in laughter. "I would never call you a horse."

Dalton planted both hands on Antoni's bum, keeping him locked inside. "Horse or not, you can ride me as many times as you like."

Now they both laughed, filling the room with their delight.

Antoni withdrew carefully, holding the condom in place until he was clear.

"The bathroom is that way," Dalton said, pointing.

Antoni nodded. He vaulted from the bed, going through the door and returning a minute later. Dalton admired the wide swing of his semi-hard cock as he walked back to the bed. Antoni flopped down beside him, and they rolled together, hugging face to face. His breath was fast against Dalton's skin. He had wiped his brow but sweat still glistened in the dark strands of his hair.

"Even after last night, I thought I was still a long way from reaching this stage," Antoni said. His hand rested on the curve of Dalton's waist.

"What changed?"

"I guess you did. You changed my attitude, I mean. And I came to realise that life is too short to put things off for too long. That man stole enough from me. It's time for me to take back control."

"I'm glad. But don't put too much pressure on yourself. Things can often take a long time to resolve themselves. Don't race into anything you're not ready for."

"I know," he said, before meeting Dalton's gaze directly again. "But I'm ready for this. I am ready for you."

He leaned closer and they kissed again. He didn't need words to convince Dalton of the message.

Chapter Sixteen

On Monday evening, Antoni left work early and drove to Morpeth, the nearest large town to Nyemouth, to visit the Polish store there. He'd asked Dalton to come round to the flat for dinner that evening and was determined to cook something that represented his own heritage. Most of the food Antoni cooked was meat-heavy but he had decided on a Lazanki recipe that could be easily adapted for a vegetarian.

It was a traditional dish made with square-shaped pasta, cabbage or sauerkraut and smoked bacon. He figured he could do a tasty version by substituting the bacon with a mixed selection of mushrooms and adding paprika for smokiness. He had checked his cupboards at lunchtime and realised he had none of the ingredients. Roger didn't object to staying back to close the gallery. His girlfriend was working that evening, and he had no plans of his own.

Antoni last heard from Dalton around four o'clock, when he had texted to confirm a time for dinner. He had no further updates on Catherine.

He rushed around the store, buying the pasta shapes, sauerkraut, onions and a variety of mushrooms, together with a fresh loaf of rye bread topped with poppy seeds and an eight pack of Polish pale lager. It was all simple but would give Dalton a taste of his homeland without scaring him off.

He hurried back to the car, already excited about seeing Dalton. Dinner wouldn't take long to cook, so he should have time for a shower and change of clothes before he arrived.

Though the days were getting longer as spring approached, it was already dusk when he returned to Nyemouth. The weather had been dull all day, with no break in the leaden clouds that hung over the town. In a month from now, when the clocks went forward and springtime began in earnest, he hoped brighter days would arrive.

As he drove over the bridge to the older side of town, the sky seemed to darken further. He hadn't checked the forecast but wondered whether they were in for a storm — not that it mattered. If it held off until Dalton arrived, they could hunker down for the night with their food and each other. He smiled to himself. It sounded like a perfect night.

They had still to broach the subject of when Dalton would return home. He had told Antoni over breakfast that he would speak to his business partner that day and make arrangements to extend his stay a little longer. He wasn't specific about how long that would be — a day, two days, a week. Antoni didn't dare hope.

He turned into the narrow back lane and drove slowly over the cobbles towards the rear of the gallery. He had locked the gates to the backyard and garage before leaving and would have to get out of the car to open them and park. As he approached the rear of the building, his headlights picked out a figure, dressed all in black, standing by the gate.

He froze, jamming his foot on the brake. Suddenly, his heart was in his throat. The car doors were already locked. He did that instinctively these days as soon as he got in.

His immediate thought was that it was the man who had stabbed him the previous year.

He's back.

It was a fear that had haunted him since that night on the pier. No corpse was ever found, and though his attacker was presumed dead, without a corpse they could never be sure.

Antoni's breath was fast and shallow, though time seemed to move slowly.

He gazed through the windscreen and relaxed a fraction.

The figure was too slender, too willowy to be that man.

They wore a dark cap and had their chin tucked into a black jacket. They turned away before he could catch more than an impression, and as they hurried to the end of the lane, he was certain of a feminine quality in their movement.

Catherine?

The height and build were about right.

She disappeared around the corner before he could make out any more detail.

Antoni overcame his fear and leapt from the car. He raced to the end of the lane.

"Catherine," he yelled.

When he turned the corner, the street was empty.

She could have gone anywhere — taken the cut down to the river, the path along to the south pier, the alley heading up to South Bank. He rushed back and forth, checking them all, but it was too late. There was no one in sight.

Could it really have been her?

Who else would have reason to snoop around his back door?

But she would have to know about his relationship with Dalton to even think about looking for him there.

"Catherine," he called out one more time. "Come and talk to me."

He waited for a reply. After a minute, when none came, he returned to the car.

* * * *

"Are you sure it was her?" Dalton asked.

"No," he admitted. "I didn't see her face. It was nothing more than an impression, from her stature and the way that she moved. But I have an eye for that kind of thing. I've worked with your sister…photographed her. My instinct tells me yes. It was her."

"Shit. I knew she was up to something."

They were in the lane at the back of the gallery. As soon as Dalton had arrived, Antoni showed him where he'd seen the figure in black. The imprint of the event was still clear in his mind. "She was waiting here when I pulled up, then fled in that direction."

Dalton glanced up at the walls on either side. "Is there any CCTV around here?"

"We have cameras, but they only cover the front of the gallery and the rear entrance and back yard. They don't extend this far. I've already checked. She doesn't appear on any of them. Some of the other businesses might cover the back alley, but it will have to wait until tomorrow. I'm sure they'll let me view their footage, though."

Dalton sighed. "Thanks." His expression was downbeat. "Though there's not much point. We both know it was her."

Antoni touched his elbow. "Are you okay?"

"Sure. It just confirms what I suspected all along. This is another hoax. A trick."

"I'm sorry, though I can't say with one-hundred percent certainty it was Catherine."

"It was her. She's up to something. And she's here still — in town, or close to it. Maybe someone is helping her hide and lie low. She must have heard about the two of us, too. There's no other reason for her to snoop around your gallery."

Prior to this evening, Antoni had thought Dalton judged his sister too harshly. That, despite what Dalton claimed, her disappearance could have been legitimate. Now, he had come round to Dalton's way of thinking. Catherine was playing with her brother, and he hated the idea. He'd had more than his fair share of contact with unhinged people. He didn't need another one stalking him or his property.

"Let's go inside," he said, guiding Dalton into the yard. He locked the gate securely behind them. If Catherine came back, there was no way she was getting in.

Upstairs, in the kitchen, he opened a couple of the beers and set them on the table with glasses. Dalton poured his and took a long draught. He swallowed and licked his lips appreciatively.

Antoni opened his tablet computer and tapped through the photo gallery before handing it to Dalton. "Take a look at these."

"What are they?" Dalton asked, peering at the screen.

"It only occurred to me last night, but when you said Catherine was no longer a subject for discussion, I didn't bring it up." He leaned over Dalton's shoulder and pointed at the first image. "These are all the photos I took of her for our shoot at the beach. I wanted you to look through them."

He filled a pan of water and set it to boil while Dalton studied the images, then took out a chopping board to work on the onions and mushrooms for their meal.

"It was something you said at the restaurant that got me thinking—about the influence Catherine has over others. How soon they fall under her spell and become enraptured by her. You know, like Justin?"

"Sure. She's always had a way of wrapping certain people around her finger."

"That's what I thought. Well, she has this friend…Larissa."

"Yep. She almost tore me a new arsehole when I didn't take Catherine's disappearance seriously.

Antoni chuckled, slicing the mushrooms. "Right. Well, she came along for the photoshoot. I thought she was Catherine's PA at first, the way she ordered her around, but as I got to know her, I realised they were just friends. She's very beautiful. I suggested taking some shots of them together, but Catherine wouldn't hear of it. Said she was paying for the shoot, *blah blah blah*, and only wanted pictures of herself."

Dalton gave a little snort through his nose. "That sounds like my sister, all right."

"So, look at some of the shots I did take. The full images before I cropped them for the final prints. You'll see Larissa at the edge of the frame in a lot of them."

Dalton flicked back and forth through the screen. "Oh, yeah. Christ. You're right. She's looking at Catherine adoringly in nearly every one."

"Keep going. I reviewed the pictures this afternoon, after having the idea last night. I noticed a change in Larissa's demeanour. She goes from looking on with affection to looking very sad...hurt. I think those were taken after Catherine rejected the idea of using her in the shots. Catherine...? Well, she didn't turn Larissa down subtly. It was harsh."

"No shit. She doesn't care about anyone's feelings but her own." Dalton zoomed in on one of the photos, closing in on Larissa. "You're right. She looks upset in this one."

Antoni continued with the cooking while Dalton studied the screen. He added onions to a frying pan and turned them in oil over a slow heat. The water came to the boil, but he wasn't ready to add the pasta yet and turned the heat down.

"Do you think Larissa is in love with her?" he asked. "Or could they even be lovers?"

"I'm not sure. The thought has occurred to me. And she wouldn't be the first lover Catherine treated like shit." Dalton zoomed in on another image. "You know it wouldn't surprise me, after what I've learned about my sister this weekend. Justin... Paul... She used sex to control both of them. Why not Larissa?"

"Could Larissa be in on this? Whatever it is Catherine is up to? Maybe she's hiding out at her place."

Dalton put down the tablet and sighed. "I don't know. I wouldn't rule anything out when it comes to my sister. Anything is possible. And she's a master at getting people to do what she wants." He looked up at Antoni. "Hey... Could it have been Larissa you saw tonight? Maybe she was snooping around on her behalf."

"I'm not sure," Antoni said, stirring the onions. He'd already convinced himself the figure in black was Catherine. "Maybe. It was dark. They have a similar build, I suppose. It could have been, but I don't know."

Dalton got up from the table and came up behind Antoni. He slid his hands around his waist and rested his chin on his shoulder. "Ah, fuck 'em. Catherine is dominating our conversation again, and I came here to be with you. What are you making, anyway?"

Antoni turned his head for a kiss. "It's a surprise. Won't be long, though. Let's finish these beers while it's cooking."

Dalton was right. Catherine Caine was like a black cloud hanging over everything they did. They needed to forget her. Their time together was running out, and they needed to make the most of every moment.

* * * *

The following morning was beautiful, with a clear, pale blue sky. Antoni suggested a walk along the beach before going into town for breakfast. There was frost on the cobbles when they left the flat. Dalton had come over last night in a lightweight jacket. Antoni lent him a sweater, together with a scarf and gloves for their early morning excursion.

"I didn't bring the right kind of clothes for this climate," Dalton said as they walked down the back alley. "It's nowhere near as chilly as this back home."

"It'll warm up by midday," Antoni assured him. "It's just the mornings that are cold at this time of year."

"I'll have to go shopping at some point today. I'm running out of clean underwear."

They both laughed. "Bring your used stuff over to mine later. You can put it in the washing machine." They still hadn't discussed how long Dalton intended to stay in Nyemouth. It was a tricky subject, and Antoni had been cautious about bringing it up. The current conversation seemed like the ideal time to raise it. "When do you think you'll go home?"

"I spoke to Allegra yesterday. She was great and told me to take as long as I needed. She says she can manage on her own. I've been helping remotely when I'm able. An hour here and there, but I can't leave it all to her. I don't know. I might have to go back by the end of the week if there's no news here."

Antoni forced a smile. The update was like a blow to the heart, but he didn't want Dalton to feel under any obligation to him. They had both known what they were getting into from the start. They lived at opposite ends of the country from each other. This couldn't be any more than it was right now.

"Sorry," Dalton said, as though reading his mind.

"It's only Tuesday," Antoni said brightly. "Let's not worry about the end of the week until we have to."

They crossed the bridge and headed along the north bank in the direction of the pier. It had just gone eight o'clock, and most of the shops had yet to open. The sea beyond the harbour, though dappled with whitecaps, looked calm, and most of the fishing boats had gone out for the day. There was an empty berth where Harry's boat, *Absent Friends*, was usually docked. Antoni guessed he had taken her out to try her along the coast, given the favourable conditions today.

When they came to the point, Antoni led Dalton down onto the beach. The tide was out, and they walked along the flat, wet sand at the water's edge.

"Recognise it?" he asked.

Dalton gazed along the golden beach and upwards, over the rocky outcrop and towering cliff. "This is where you came with Catherine?"

"Yeah. We spent a couple of hours down here, taking shots all along the beach."

"It's gorgeous."

"I've always thought so. I've lived here for so long you would think I'd take it for granted by now, but I never have. I love it. I must have taken thousands of photos along this stretch of coast and no two are ever the same. It's always different, depending on the time of day, the weather, the season. I never tire of it."

Dalton took his hand. Antoni had always struggled with public displays of affection, but he accepted Dalton's hand without a sense of awkwardness. It felt entirely right for them to walk along like this on a cold spring morning. He grinned and drew the sharp air deep into his lungs. He was sharing his favourite place with a man who had changed his life for the better. It was all he could have hoped for.

"I can see why you love it," Dalton said. "What a privilege to have this on your doorstep, to be able to take walks like this whenever you want to." He came closer and put his arm around Antoni. He pressed a warm kiss to his cold cheek. "Thanks for sharing it with me."

Despite the chill air and the breeze from the sea, Antoni had never felt warmer.

"I wish I'd brought my camera, so I could take some pictures of you."

"I don't know about your fancy cameras, but I'm good for a selfie." Dalton tugged off a glove and dug in his pocket, producing two phones.

"Two?" Antoni asked.

"Afraid so. I'm one of *those* people—personal *and* business." Dalton shoved one back in his pocket. "I don't like to share my personal number with clients. I learned the hard way that they will call you any time they like, day or night. I give them the work number, and I switch it off at evenings and weekends. Got to have some boundaries." He pulled Antoni even closer, holding the phone in front of them. "Smile."

He didn't even have to ask. Antoni couldn't contain the smile that covered his entire face.

By nine o'clock they were both feeling a little peckish and headed back into town. The traffic through the harbour area was still light, but a few of the shops had opened since they'd passed on the way out.

"I'm desperate for a coffee," Dalton said. "My feet are absolutely freezing. I need to warm up. Where shall we go?"

"The Seagull is the best at this time of day."

There were a few empty tables inside when they arrived. Antoni gestured for Dalton to grab one in the corner. "I'll place the order. What would you like?"

"A cappuccino would be good."

"What about breakfast?"

"I'm not all that hungry. Just a pastry or a croissant. I don't mind. Whatever they have."

With a grin, Antoni headed for the counter. Dalton's phone rang as he walked away. *Work, no doubt.* He hoped Dalton's business partner hadn't changed their mind about him staying as long as he liked and needed him back sooner.

There were three people in the line in front of him. Antoni got lost in his thoughts, thinking about last night and the walk this morning, until it was his turn. He placed Dalton's order and got a breakfast tea and sausage sandwich for himself.

Dalton had both elbows on the table when he returned, his head hung forward. Antoni knew in an instant that something was wrong.

"What is it?" he asked, sliding into the seat.

When Dalton lifted his head, his face was ashen. He raised his phone and said, "I just got a call from the police."

The warmth that had permeated all through Antoni vanished. His blood turned to ice.

"Someone found a body on a beach this morning, several miles down the coast. They... They think it could be my sister."

Chapter Seventeen

Dalton collected Justin from home and drove south. He had entered the hospital postcode into the route planner and followed the directions automatically, without much active thought. He had called his parents on his way to Justin's house and given them what little information he knew. They had both sounded shocked. Like him, they had made light of Catherine's disappearance, and this morning's development was beyond anything they had previously experienced. He had promised to update them as soon as he knew more.

Justin said little on the journey. Unlike yesterday, he was clean and dressed and smelled of soap and aftershave. His gaze was fixed firmly ahead. Dalton doubted he was focused on the road, and his thoughts were all turned inwards.

Did I get this so wrong?

From the beginning, Justin had been worried about Catherine, while Dalton was dismissive of the whole situation. Dalton had been quick to judge his sister, based on past experiences, where Justin had shown nothing but concern.

Before setting off, they had pooled their knowledge of the small details the police had given them. The naked body of a woman had been found on the beach by a dog walker, several miles down the coast from where Catherine had gone missing. The age and general description of the woman was consistent with Catherine, and the police had requested a formal identification.

Had she really gone through with it? After all these years of false alarms and attention-seeking behaviour, had she taken her own life?

Dalton was numb and knew he should be more upset than he was. He was in shock — yes, stunned — but there were no tears, was no grief. They would come later. For now, there was a job to be done.

Justin's eyes were dry, too. His silent, still manner made it impossible for Dalton to gauge how he was really feeling. His last words before leaving his house had been, "We don't know it's her yet?"

Wishful thinking, but if that was what he needed to get through, Dalton wouldn't take it away from him. He'd been scouring the local news pages and social media groups for days and, as far as he was aware, no other women had been reported missing along the coastline in that time. Only Catherine.

Shit.

As he drove, his mind flashed back down the years of growing up with Catherine. There had been so much distance between them from the moment he was born. They had never been close, and she had bullied Dalton and his brother Tobias from as early as he could remember. He recalled the trouble she'd had at school, all the fights with their parents, the strange days when she went missing and the police had become regular visitors to the house. It would be easy to blame their parents for the way she had turned out, but he knew they had done everything they could. There had been doctors, therapy, counselling. They had known how deeply troubled their daughter was, but nothing they put in place to help her worked. This distance between Catherine and the family had grown further. Dalton was the only one speaking to her now, and he could hardly count himself as a devoted brother.

He'd built bridges with her to ease his own guilt.

They reached the outskirts of a small town. The route planner took them on a ring road to the hospital.

Dalton's heart began to race as he pulled up and cut the engine.

"This is it," he said.

Justin got out without saying a word.

Dalton had spoken to a DS Norton that morning and had been given instructions to call his number when they arrived. The Detective Sergeant told them to go into the hospital and he would meet them in the main reception.

The hospital was much like any other he had visited — bright, functional and smelling of disinfectant. When they reached the reception, he called the detective to say they had arrived.

DS Norton was around Dalton's age, with a round face and caring eyes. He introduced his partner, DS Williams, an older man in his early fifties. Dalton didn't take in much of what they said as they were led to the morgue on a lower level. Justin kept pace beside him, still silent.

Dalton's mouth was dry. His pulse pounded in his temples. He expected there would be a viewing room, like he had seen on so many TV shows, but they were taken straight into a sterile room, where a trolley was already waiting with the body covered by a white sheet.

"Oh, my God," he gasped, close to losing it. He drew in deep breaths, trying to calm his jagged nerves. It was suddenly all very real and terrifying. His sister was lying dead under that sheet. Tears pricked his eyes, and he crammed his fist into his mouth.

"Take your time," DS Norton said. "Tell us when you're ready, and we'll remove the sheet. You just have to tell us if it's Catherine or not. We should warn you that she's been in the water, and she won't look exactly as you remember. So, prepare yourself for that."

Dalton looked at Justin. His mouth was pinched, otherwise his expression was completely vacant. He was in shock. Dalton knew it was up to him to do this. He took another moment to compose himself, summoned saliva to his dry mouth then said, "All right, I'm ready."

A morgue attendant carefully raised the sheet from the face.

Dalton took another breath and forced himself to look.

The first thing he noticed was a tangle of damp, tawny blond hair. The skin was greyish blue, but the features, the nose, the mouth were all wrong. It was not his sister.

"It's not her," he blurted.

"What?" Justin, who had been looking the other way, stepped forward.

"That's not Catherine," Dalton said to the police officers.

They exchanged a glance.

"No," said Justin, finding his voice. "It's Larissa Crawford."

Startled, Dalton turned back to the body. All he'd taken in was enough to determine that the dead woman wasn't Catherine. He forced himself to look closer. He had only met Larissa once and seen the pictures Antoni had taken. It was difficult to compare the lifeless corpse on the trolley to that beautiful woman, but as he studied her face, the features began to match.

"You know her?" DS Norton asked, suddenly very alert.

"Yes," Justin said. "It's Larissa Crawford. She's one of Catherine's friends."

* * * *

Antoni was talking to a customer and explaining the location for one of his photographs when a familiar tightness came across his chest. The man, a tourist from Holland, showed great interest in the landscape and was keen to know where the image had been taken. Antoni took a deep breath and tried to continue.

"It's along the coast, about two miles from here. If you follow the walking trail along the top of North Point, you'll come to it, eventually. There's a good path and it's well signposted. You can't miss it."

His guts had twisted, seeming to crush his entire torso, forcing his heart and his lungs into an ever-constricted space. He recognised the signs. His hands clenched into fists. He forced them to uncurl and wiped his palms on his trousers, hoping the customer hadn't noticed. There was a raging thunder in his head as blood pounded through his brain. His chest grew tight, and it became harder to breathe.

"Ethan can show you on the map," he said, managing to control the tremor in his voice. He guided the man to the counter. "Ethan, would you show this gentleman how he can find the walking trails?" He swallowed, his mouth bone dry.

Ethan caught his eyes, and an unspoken message passed between them. The younger man recognised what was happening.

"Sure," he said, pulling a guidebook from beneath the desk. He made a big deal of distracting the customer.

Antoni hurried to the stock room. His pulse pounded in his temples, and it was harder than ever to catch a breath. The room seemed to close around him, the ceiling lowering. He dropped to his haunches, clutching his hands before him, and focused on slowing everything down.

Count, he told himself. *One, two, three*. One breath after another, that was all that mattered.

It was his first serious anxiety attack in weeks, but he knew the signs well enough. They were a familiar enemy.

It took the best part of ten minutes to get it under control, by which time he had a terrible headache that threatened to progress into a migraine. He switched out the light and lay on the settee, one arm covering his eyes to block out the remaining light. He drew breaths deep into his diaphragm, in through his nose and out through his mouth.

This is not the worst. You can handle it.

Roger came to see him half an hour later. "How are you?" he asked, leaving the lights off.

"Better," Antoni answered, staying where he was.

"Ethan told me what happened. Did it come on from nowhere?"

He sighed. "Pretty much." He had learned the hard way that anxiety attacks didn't always require a trigger. It was easy to avoid violent TV shows or movies that might bring back difficult memories. Large crowds were a problem, but one he found simple enough to avoid. When he had first returned to work at the gallery, an irrational fear of strangers had been a massive issue. Even now, he minimised his front-of-house contact to one or two hours a day. But at other times, the attacks came from nowhere…like today. Antoni hadn't felt threatened or intimidated by the customer, but the tightness of the chest and difficulty breathing had come on him just the same.

"All this stuff about Catherine Caine can't be helping," Roger said.

Roger was never one to beat about the bush.

"The body on the beach isn't Catherine," Antoni reminded him.

"But you knew the girl. She was part of Catherine's set. It's a lot to take in, for anyone."

Antoni wanted to tell Roger he was wrong and being overprotective, but it was no good. Of course, the stresses of the last few days had had an influence on him and had more than likely, no, certainly, triggered the latest panic attack. "I can handle it."

Roger's voice came closer in the dark. "Is it worth the risk? When you've been doing so well. This business with the sister could set you back weeks."

Antoni took four long, deep breaths then said, "I'm willing to take the chance. Dalton has done so much for my confidence, for my own mental health since we met on Friday. I can't explain how different I feel because of him. I don't want to abandon him now."

"I'm not suggesting you abandon him, but he knows what you've been through. I'm sure he'll understand if you step aside and avoid the worst of it."

"I'm sure he will, too," Antoni said, "but I won't ask him to, because I don't want to. I want to be with him and support him through this, whatever happens."

He sensed his brother brooding in the darkness.

"Don't worry about me," Antoni continued.

"You can say that, but I do, little brother. Ever since I got the call that Sunday to say you were hurt and in the hospital, I've done nothing but worry."

"I know. But I wish you wouldn't. Please."

Roger sighed.

Antoni opened his eyes and made out the shape of his brother in the gloom. His head didn't hurt so much now. With luck, he had managed to avoid the full-on wrath of a migraine. He slowly rose into a sitting position. The room no longer felt the size of a shoebox. "I'm okay."

"Can I do something?" Roger asked.

Antoni laughed softly. "That kind of depends on what it is."

"Let me ask Indina about the investigation." Roger's girlfriend was a police officer.

"Is she even involved in the case? She could get into trouble if she told you something they don't want the public to know."

"No, she's not involved, but she could find out. I'm sure of it. She tells me about other investigations. I don't see why this is different."

"Because you're involved, however tenuously. No. I don't think it's a good idea. It's not worth the trouble it could cause her."

"Let her be the judge of that, eh? She doesn't have to tell me anything she doesn't want to. And besides, it will go no further than you and me. What harm could it do?"

Antoni realised his brother had already made up his mind. He would quiz Indina about the investigation whether he approved it or not. And maybe Roger was right. They had a contact in the police force. What harm could there be in gaining a little inside information?

The situation was getting murkier by the day. If Roger's girlfriend could shed a little light, it could be better for everyone.

"Okay," he said. "Ask her, but don't make a big deal. If she says she doesn't want to do it, leave it at that. I'm serious."

"Sure," Roger said. "You have my word."

Chapter Eighteen

Dalton lay on his side with Antoni's body wrapped around the curve of his spine. Physically and mentally, he was exhausted. It had been the most stressful day in his already nerve-racking visit to Nyemouth, but sleep was the last thing on his mind. Lying with Antoni, his arm draped protectively around Dalton, was the safest and most secure he had felt all day. It was after eleven. Despite his tiredness, his senses were bizarrely alert. He could hear the river lapping against the harbour beneath the bedroom window, voices of people farther along the marina as the pubs emptied for the night, a television playing in one of the nearby hotel rooms.

He had met Antoni earlier in the evening for dinner in the bar. Dalton could barely remember what either of them had eaten. They had sat in one of the booths, mindlessly picking at their food while Dalton recounted everything that had happened – from the phone call that morning, to the visit to the morgue and all that had occurred since. He'd spent most of the afternoon with Justin, who had been quiet and withdrawn throughout. Dalton had struggled to find any words to comfort Justin, knowing how removed his own thoughts and suspicions must be from what Justin was thinking.

They had overheard the usual Nyemouth gossip as they went to the bar to get served. The people in this town seemed to thrive on death and chaos.

Dalton took a deep breath through his nose. It came out as a sigh.

"Can't you sleep?" Antoni asked softly.

"No. I can't seem to turn off my brain. There's just too much stuff going around and around in there. The sound of it is almost deafening."

Antoni stroked his belly. "I know what that's like."

Dalton rolled onto his back and propped an arm behind his head. He stared at the ceiling. He heard gunfire and explosions from the TV in one of the other rooms. "Sounds like an action movie," he remarked.

"Probably. Put the TV on if you think it will help. Sometimes a distraction like that is just what you need."

"I don't think so. I'm trying to get my head straight. More noise is unlikely to help."

Antoni rose onto his elbow beside him. "I used to think like that, but you'd be surprised what turned out to be useful. I keep a stack of cookery books beside my bed for the nights I can't sleep. Planning meals and thinking about what I want to cook is one of the things I find most relaxing."

Dalton gave another great sigh. "Fuck. I'm sorry. My head is such a mess tonight."

"Hey, don't apologise. After the day you've had, I can't think of a single person who wouldn't be in a state right now. How you feel is perfectly normal. Trust me."

After a long moment, he said, "I've never seen a dead body before, let alone someone in that condition. It was awful. I've heard when people have been in the water that it's not a pleasant sight, but whoa. Nothing prepared me for that. It was only later, after I'd recovered from the shock of it not being Catherine, that it really hit me." He turned his head to look at Antoni in the shadowy light of the room. "Have you? Seen a dead person, I mean?"

He nodded. "It's never pleasant under any circumstance, let alone what you're talking about." He moved his hand across Dalton's bare torso until it rested on his chest, right above his heart. "Is that what's troubling you tonight? Because the shock of seeing Larissa like that will fade eventually. It'll take time."

He returned his gaze to the ceiling, staring at the uneven surface. "I wish that's all it was," he said at last. Could he even articulate what really troubled him? He had to try. "It's Catherine. Her story is still ongoing, only it has taken a far darker turn."

"You don't know that. What happened to Larissa might just be a coincidence."

"It's not." He thumped his guts. "I feel it in here. You said yourself that there might have been something between the two of them."

"That was only a suspicion. I don't know for sure. It was just a feeling I got."

"I'm sure—because that's what my sister does. She draws people to her and toys with them, like a cat with a mouse, until she's bored or devises a new plan. She's cunning like that."

"You make her sound like a female Hannibal Lecter."

"It's not a bad comparison."

"You can't be serious."

"I am. Catherine is dangerous. I think we've had it wrong, believing all this time that she was a danger to herself. That's not right. She's a risk to other people."

"Dalton, you're upset. After what you've been through, it's understandable. But no one knows what happened to Larissa yet."

"I have a pretty good idea. Well, a good suspicion. Something happened to me today, after I saw the body. It loosened something inside. Maybe you would call it triggering, but it made me think about something that happened years ago, when we were kids. When *I* was a kid. It's always been there, really—at the back of my mind, packed away—but I finally acknowledged it today for what it really was."

Antoni shifted in bed beside him, shuffling into a sitting position. "Do you want to tell me about it? Can you?"

When Dalton turned to look at him, he saw Antoni through a blur and realised there were tears in his eyes. Then it came out of him in a tumble. Long forgotten, buried recollections burst to the surface.

Summer holidays with his family were some of his fondest memories of growing up. His parents were comfortable in their finances, but they were never extravagant. The family would enjoy one good holiday each year, two weeks every summer, and that was it. Unlike other kids he knew, there were no spring skiing trips or winter escapes to the sun. He didn't need them. He had never been jealous of his friends, because he had the best time with his own family—his parents, Tobias, even Catherine's behaviour became more tolerable when they were away.

Each summer his parents would rent a villa, usually in the south of France, but other times in Spain or Portugal.

It was one of those years in Spain that had returned to haunt him.

The villa had been a wonderland for a boy of seven. It stood on a hill, overlooking a horseshoe-shaped bay, spread over three floors with balconies in each of the bedrooms, a large garden terrace and its own swimming pool. Dalton remembered spending more time in that pool, splashing around on inflatable beds and toys than anything else.

"My skin must have been permanently water-logged," he told Antoni.

"You were seven. So Catherine was what? Thirteen, then?"

He nodded. "Yeah. Tobias would have been around ten. It's been coming back to me in pieces all afternoon. I mean, I already remembered the holiday and even a little of what happened that day, but not all of it — not until now." Two slow, hot tears rolled down the sides of his face. He wiped them away.

The memory was vivid now, like it had only happened yesterday.

Tobias had been asleep in the shade of the veranda, sprawled on his back with a baseball cap covering his face. His mother and father had been making plans for dinner that evening when a couple who were staying in the villa next door came to call. All four of the adults had been around the front, talking at the gate. Dalton had been floating on an inflatable raft. He remembered moving up and down the pool, pretending he was one of the kids from *Jaws*, trying to avoid the killer shark. He would suddenly put on a great burst of speed, flying the full length of the pool to avoid the imaginary beast.

"You're such a geek," Catherine had said. She had been sitting at the edge, her legs submerged, watching him with ill-disguised derision. *"You should see the state of you. My God, it's pathetic."*

Dalton had kept moving, pretending to take no notice of her comments. He was used to them. When their parents were out of earshot, Catherine loved to hurl criticism at her brothers. And like all the other times, she refused to be ignored.

"You're only on that thing because you're scared of the water," she'd said.

Dalton remembered burning with anger. Why did she have to belittle everything he did?

"No, I'm not."

"You can't even swim. You're such a baby."

"Shut up. I can swim...better than you."

She had scoffed at that. *"I don't fucking think so."* She would always swear when their parents weren't around. Catherine had slipped from the edge into the water, her thin body barely causing a ripple.

Dalton had paddled in the opposite direction, undeterred. She swam after him.

"Come on then. Prove it," she'd said. *"If you're such a hot fucking swimmer, get off that baby toy and show me."*

She had been in one of those moods. He knew it well. She wouldn't stop tormenting him until his humiliation was complete.

"Leave me alone," he'd said. *"I'll tell on you."*

He had reached the far end of the pool...the deep end. He shuffled around, trying to push off against the side and turn around.

Catherine had grabbed his leg. *"Come on, baby. Didn't you just tell me what a great swimmer you are? If you're such hot shit, why are you scared to prove it?"*

"I'm not scared," he'd said, trying to navigate the raft around her. She still had a grip on his ankle. *"I don't want to. Let me be."*

"Let me be," she'd mimicked.

He'd known he was in trouble. The bullying wouldn't stop until his parents returned. He'd raised his head, looking up the garden, hoping to see them coming back. There was no sign.

With a fierce yank, Catherine had torn him from the raft. Completely submerged, he had swallowed water before clawing his way to the surface, coughing and gasping for air.

Catherine's eyes had sparkled with a dark glee. *"Not such a strong swimmer after all."*

Before he could respond, her hands were on his shoulders, and she had pushed him down again. He had managed to gasp a short breath before going under. Her grip had been relentless, digging into his young flesh, manipulating her weight from above to hold him down. He had batted at her hands and wrists, trying to free himself, but a skinny seven-year-old was no match for a wily teenager.

His lungs had ached, and he'd fought desperately against the instinct to inhale.

Looking upwards, he'd made out the shape of her head above the water, her long dark hair flowing around her. And through the rippling surface he'd seen her terrible grin.

Despite every effort, his struggles had weakened, and that distorted smile had been the last thing he remembered before darkness overcame him.

"Oh my God." Antoni held him as his body trembled. The trauma of the memory threatened to overwhelm him. It had coalesced in his brain all day, but it was only now, saying it out loud to someone else, that the true impact of what had happened hit him. "She tried to *kill* you? As a *child?*"

"I'm certain of it. I think deep down, I've always known it. That repressed memory is the thing that's always made me keep her at a distance."

"But what happened? Your parents must have known."

"They came back to find me in the pool. My dad pulled me out. It wasn't too late. He was able to revive me."

"What about Catherine? How did she get out of that?"

"She told them I had fallen off the raft into the deep end. That she'd been trying to rescue me when they returned. It's a good job they came back when they did. Another minute and it would have been too late."

"They believed her?"

"I guess so. What choice did they have? No one witnessed what really happened, and I must have been too traumatised to tell the truth. I don't know. I could be remembering it wrong, but I think my mother's attitude towards Catherine shifted after that incident. I think she suspected. She certainly became more protective towards us two boys after that holiday."

Antoni held him for a long time. Neither of them said anything. The tears eventually stopped and were replaced by a dull numbness.

My sister tried to kill me.

She would have passed it off as a tragic accident.

Like Larissa?

"I don't think it's safe for you to be here," Antoni said at last.

"Why?"

"Given what you've just told me, and the fact I thought I saw Catherine behind the gallery last night, the night before Larissa turned up dead, I don't think it's wise for you to stay."

"I'm not ready to go. I won't let her drive me away from you."

"Can you take the risk? I don't want to believe it myself — it sounds unbelievable — but I have the scars to prove that nothing is impossible. Your sister is dangerous, and if she's still around, you should get as far away from her as you can."

Dalton shuffled up the bed, propping himself up. "I'm not a seven-year-old kid anymore. I'm not afraid of her. Whatever it is she has planned, I want to know what it is, and I want to expose her for the sake of everyone she's ever hurt. Her ex-boyfriend Paul, with the iron burn on his chest, that's probably a fraction of the hurt she's caused over the years. For the sake of my family, and for me, I want to reveal her for the monster that she is."

Chapter Nineteen

Antoni returned to the flat for a shower and a change of clothes before opening the gallery and shop. He'd been reluctant to leave Dalton behind, but Roger wasn't due in until late, and it was Ethan's day off. He had no option other than to go to work. Dalton had assured him he would be fine. He planned to go for a run to clear his head and get his thoughts in order. He'd said he needed some time on his own.

Antoni didn't push it. He knew how claustrophobic it could be when someone needed space and well-intentioned family and friends insisted on staying close. If Dalton said he wanted to be alone, Antoni believed him.

Dalton had fallen asleep sometime after two, though it had been far from restful. He had thrashed around the bed, moaning and crying for the rest of the night. Lying beside him, Antoni had slept even less. Nights were the worst time for him, anyway. There was no point in forcing sleep when he knew it wouldn't come.

That morning he had been conflicted. As he stood in the shower, waiting for the hot water to bring his tired body back to life, he'd relived everything they had talked about the previous night. Antoni had not changed his mind. As much as it would hurt to see Dalton leave, it seemed like the only safe option. Catherine Caine was a danger to her brother. Not a physical danger — he hoped to God that was true — but she was a definite emotional threat. If what Dalton suspected was true and this was all part of an elaborate mind game, then her younger brother was the focus of it. The best thing was for Dalton to leave Nyemouth and deny her the satisfaction of fulfilling her plans.

If Dalton left it would crush Antoni, but it was better than the alternative of some serious harm coming to him. The longer he stayed, the more likely that would be.

Dalton Caine had changed his life for the better in just a few days, but Antoni would sacrifice it all to keep Dalton safe.

Once dressed, he went downstairs and opened the gallery. Between online orders and a smattering of tourists, he had enough to keep busy and occupy his thoughts until Roger came in at noon.

"Got you a coffee," Roger announced, carrying in two takeaway cups.

"Thanks. I'm ready for it."

Roger looked at him closely. "Tired?"

"I'm always tired," Antoni reminded him, taking the lid off his coffee cups to let out some of the heat. "Getting by on almost no sleep will do that."

"Have you had any further panic attacks?"

"No. Just what happened yesterday. I'm sure it was a one-off. It wasn't that bad, anyway."

"It's one too many, little brother."

"I'm fine," Antoni assured him. Roger could make a fuss when he didn't want it, but Antoni appreciated how much he cared. He couldn't imagine any circumstance where he would do something to hurt Roger — or vice versa. The notion of one sibling trying to drown another in a swimming pool was abhorrent. Beyond that, it was evil. Although Dalton had repressed the memory for most of his life, it was no surprise he had such a distrust of his sister.

Roger cast his eye around the shop and into the gallery. Satisfied there were no customers, he said, "So, I spoke to Indina last night about Larissa Crawford."

Antoni's flesh prickled. Was he about to open a door he might not be able to close again? For Dalton's sake, he would have to take the risk. "Was she able to tell you anything?"

Roger hesitated, as though weighing up the pros and cons of revealing what he knew.

"Come on," Antoni said. "You've already caused your girlfriend to break professional confidentiality. You might as well let me in on the secret, too."

Roger widened his eyes. "Damn. Okay, you're right. Well, she couldn't tell me much. She's not involved in the investigation, but when something big like this happens, it seems it's the talk of the police station. Right? Everyone is asking about it." He pulled out the stool behind the counter and sat. "Larissa was already dead when she went into the water. She didn't drown."

The news hit Antoni like a blow to the guts, and all the horrors of the last year came crashing back. There were so many similarities to his own case — suspicious deaths, a victim disposed of in the sea. "What do they think happened?"

"It's a murder investigation," Roger said flatly. "Larissa had an injury to the back of her head. They needed an autopsy to confirm it for sure. It's the kind of thing that could have happened while she was in the water. You know, smashed against the rocks as the tide carried the body along the coast."

"And the police don't think that's what happened?"

Roger shook his head. "There's no doubt. The blunt trauma was caused before she went in. It was a hammer blow. Someone struck her over the head with a hammer then dumped her body in the sea."

Antoni's legs weakened. He gripped the counter. "And do they know when?"

"She had only been in the water around ten hours before she was found, which means she was killed the night before last—sometime before eleven o'clock."

The night he'd seen Catherine in the back alley.

* * * *

The tide was low and the wet sand at the bottom of the beach made for a firm if strenuous running ground. Dalton embraced the challenge. He hadn't done any real exercise in over a week. It was a cool morning with a brisk wind coming from the north, and he powered headlong into it, allowing his mind to clear as his body coped with the physical trial.

It was somewhere along this beach that Catherine's clothes had been found on Saturday morning. He didn't know where and cared even less. His sister wasn't missing. She was in hiding. He had no doubt of that now. He wouldn't let her actions spoil his enjoyment of a good run.

As Catherine crept back into his thoughts, he increased his pace, pushing his body further, ignoring the burn in his thigh muscles and the stitch in his side. He had passed two women walking their dogs when he'd first come down the ramp from the town, but since then, he'd had the beach to himself.

The things Antoni had said last night preyed on his mind, telling him to leave town for his own safety. Antoni hadn't asked him to go from any desire to curtail their burgeoning relationship. Dalton was certain of that. Antoni's feelings were as strong as his own. It was the risk he thought Catherine posed. Antoni was right in one respect. Dalton also believed he was at the centre of Catherine's scheming. He'd suspected he might have been all along, probably from the moment he'd agreed to come to her damned party.

But until he'd spoken to Paul the other day and identified Larissa's body, he'd failed to appreciate how dangerous she was.

Despite the scars on Paul's chest and his own memories of that day in the pool, it was still a struggle to accept that Catherine had had something to do with her friend's death, but he didn't find it impossible, either.

Nobody knew what she was capable of, except herself.

He had reached the end of the beach. A large outcrop of jagged rock extended into the sea. It was too rugged for him to climb, and there was no other way around it. He paused for a moment to catch his breath. Sweat poured over his brow, and he wiped it on his sleeve. He wasn't ready to quit. When he got back to town, he would see if there was a way up onto the cliffs, and he would run the same distance again from above. The exercise had helped his mood, and he wasn't ready to give up yet.

His phone rang as he was about to start back.

It was Justin. He considered rejecting the call. How deep was Justin involved in this whole mess? Could he be Catherine's accomplice or another innocent stooge?

Dalton answered. "Hey."

"Oh, hi. Are you okay? You sound out of breath."

"I'm running," he told him.

"Oh, right. Have the police spoken to you yet?"

"When? You mean today? No."

"They will. They came here first thing."

He waited for Justin to elaborate. *What the hell is this? It's like pulling bloody teeth.* "And?" he asked, hearing the irritation in his own voice.

"They wanted to know about Larissa. How well I knew her? How well she knew Catherine? When was the last time I saw her alive? Dalton, they believe she was murdered."

Shit. His worst suspicions had become a reality. "What did you tell them? How well *did* she know Catherine?"

"They were friends, that's all. What do you think I said? Wait. Hang on... You don't think Catherine has been murdered, too, do you?" The tone of Justin's voice went from calm to hysterical in seconds. "Do you think whoever killed Larissa has also done something to Catherine?"

Dalton turned to the sea, calming himself with deep, salty breaths. The surface of the water was choppy, with deeper waves and whitecaps farther out.

"No," he said, deflated. "I don't think Catherine is dead. I think the same as I've always done, that she's hiding somewhere, waiting to make her move."

"Oh, man. That doesn't make any sense."

It does to me. A fucking lot of sense.

"What about Larissa? You said they suspect murder."

"They do. They think someone killed her and dumped her body into the sea."

Fingers of ice gripped his spine. All his worst suspicions were taking shape.

"Did they say anything else about Catherine? The police?"

"No. Just that they hadn't found her yet. I don't even think they're seriously looking anymore."

No, he thought. *There's no need. Catherine will find us when she's ready.*

Chapter Twenty

DS Norton and DS Williams were waiting outside Quay House when Dalton returned. After the phone call from Justin, he'd headed straight back to the hotel instead of continuing his run along the cliffs.

"I heard," he told them as he approached. "Justin called and told me."

Neither of the detectives showed a trace of emotion.

"We'd like to ask you some questions and clarify a few points," DS Norton said. He wore a shirt and tie beneath a large winter coat, which swamped his portly frame. Yesterday Dalton had estimated they were around the same age, but today the police officer appeared much younger.

He nodded. "Can we go inside?"

The bar had only been open a few minutes, and there were no other customers. Dalton asked for a large glass of water before joining the two men at a table by the door. The bartender watched with interest. Dalton consciously lowered his voice when he spoke. This meeting would no doubt be passed along the

Nyemouth grapevine soon enough, but he wouldn't make it easy for the local gossips.

"I understand this is now a murder investigation," he said quietly.

"That's right," Norton said matter-of-factly.

"What can you tell us about Larissa Crawford?" DS Williams asked.

Dalton had decided on the jog back that he was done with secrets and protecting his sister. "About Larissa, almost nothing. I told you before that I only met her the one time, and that she's a friend of Catherine's. How close they were, I don't know that, either, but there's something I've since found out. A friend of mine, who worked with both Catherine and Larissa, has a feeling that their friendship might have been more than that. He thinks they could have been romantically linked. No, that's probably the wrong word. There might have been something sexual between them."

DS Williams tightened his jaw, causing a sudden twitch in his left cheek. "What evidence does your friend have of this?"

"He doesn't. I told you, it's just a feeling. But there are photographs of the two of them together. He showed them to me, and I must admit it does look like there was something between them."

"Photographs?"

"Not the kind you're thinking of. It's just some shots of the two of them from the day they worked together, but there's definitely *something* there. I just think they might have known each other better than anyone thought."

"What makes you so sure?" Norton fixed him in a stare. His eyes were soft, but the intent behind them was anything but. "Catherine and Larissa were both in relationships with men."

"All right," he said, lowering his voice further. "This is going to sound way out there, but I think Catherine might have had something to do with Larissa's death." He told the detectives everything he knew in as concise and linear a method as he could, but even as he spoke, he realized how incredible it sounded. He gave them Catherine's history of false disappearances and emotional mind games — her ability to manipulate people, her anger problems. He told them about her ex-boyfriend Paul and the scars on his chest, and how her staff had all felt the hard end of her temper. He omitted the part about her trying to drown him in a pool in Spain when they were children. Given that the memory had only come back to him the day before, he was aware of how unreliable it would sound.

When he finished, the detectives were silent. He caught a brief exchange between them, just a fraction of a side glance.

"I know it sounds crazy," he said, "but you don't understand Catherine like I do." He shook his head. "No, strike that remark. I don't think anyone understands her."

DS Norton was the first to speak. "That's quite an opinion you have about your sister."

"If you speak to my family, they'll back most of it up. Obviously, they don't know what's gone on while she's been living here, but they'll corroborate the historical parts."

"We already have," Norton stated. "And they do. Your mother in particular thinks Catherine's disappearance is a sham."

"I'm sure of it, too. More than ever now."

Thom Collins

"But what makes you so certain?"

"You need to speak to Antoni Nowak. He owns the gallery on the other side of the river."

DS Williams scribbled in his notebook. "And why is that?"

"He thinks he saw my sister...the night before last, the night Larissa was killed. It was all very fast, and he didn't see her clearly, but he's around ninety-percent sure that he saw Catherine in the alley behind the gallery."

"We haven't had a report of this."

"He didn't report it. Like I said, he's not one hundred percent. His CCTV cameras don't cover the back street. He was going to check with some of his neighbours, but I don't know how far he got."

"What time was this?"

"About quarter to eight...ten to."

Norton jerked his thumb to Williams.

"On it," DS Williams said, getting up, already on his phone before he reached the door.

"So, you believe me?" Dalton asked.

Norton grimaced. "We don't have enough evidence for that, but it's a line of enquiry we're keen to follow."

Relief surged through him. *Oh, thank God.* He wasn't crazy or on some insane vendetta against his sister.

"We've spoken to a lot of people already, including Paul Madden. What he told us matches with what he said to you, about the domestic violence within their relationship. He also showed us the scars. If Catherine returns, Paul is prepared to make a statement and press charges against her. Your sister has a lot of friends and followers who adore everything she does, but she also made a lot of enemies who are prepared to tell a different story. Right now, the evidence and statements are stacking up towards the latter."

"Is there anything I can do to help?"

"Stop keeping secrets," the detective said. "If you hear or see anything... If she makes another surprise appearance from the shadows, we need to know about it before anyone else gets hurt."

* * * *

The police didn't finish with Antoni until after eight o'clock. Norton and Williams had questioned him about what he'd seen on Monday evening, and he did his best to convince them that although he hadn't seen Catherine's face, he had an eye for figure and movement, and remained certain that she was the one he'd seen at the back gate. They had also sent a couple of uniformed detectives around to neighbouring businesses to see if they had any clearer images on their CCTV.

"That's her, for sure," he'd told them when they showed him footage from the building next door. Their camera was higher placed than his own and at a steeper angle, but it caught the figure in black as she came along the lane. She had paused at the rear of his property and tried the locked gates just moments before he'd come home.

"You still can't see her face," DS Norton argued. "She's covered up the whole time."

"It's her. Show this clip to anyone who knows her, and they'll say the same."

The detective appeared unconvinced. "Well, if what you say is true and that is indeed Catherine Caine, we need to find out exactly where she went from here."

It wouldn't be easy. Nyemouth was an old town with dozens of narrow alleys and side streets that were blind as far as CCTV coverage went. Catherine could have gone in so many directions, and they would never know it. They would have to check every private residence to see if she'd been picked up on their security systems.

"What about her bar?" he suggested. "It's less than ten minutes' walk from here. Could she be hiding out in there?"

"We searched the place this afternoon," DS Williams had told him. "If she was there, there's no sign of her now."

They were taking it all a lot more seriously. The cops had to think there was a connection between Catherine's disappearance and Larissa's murder.

Roger stuck close by Antoni for the rest of the day. Even when they had closed the gallery, he seemed reluctant to leave. "Why don't you come home with me?" he suggested. "Just for tonight."

"I'm fine. You don't have to worry."

"It was only yesterday that you had the panic attack. PTSD is a complicated thing. You know that. We both do. I think it would be better if you weren't alone."

He meant well. Antoni appreciated it, but he didn't need this special treatment. "I'm tired. I've been talking to the police for most of the day. I'm not going to be good company tonight. I just want to lock the door and be by myself for a little while."

Roger wasn't the kind of man to back down easily. "It will be just the two of us. Indina is working, anyway. We can have a few beers and some takeaway food. You can get an early night at my place if you're that tired.

But it will be better to have someone with you, don't you think?"

He shook his head. "We've been over this a million times before. I need my independence."

"You've got it all wrong. That's not what I mean. Look... We don't have a clue what's going on with this guy Dalton or his crazy sister, but none of it sounds good. She's already been creeping around your flat once this week that you know about. Why take an unnecessary risk, eh? She's not going to bother you at my place."

Antoni had heard enough. He put a gentle hand on Roger's arm and walked him to the door. "I know you mean well, brother, so let's not argue, okay? Go home, have a good night and I'll see you in the morning. Nothing is going to happen to me between now and then."

Roger looked like he was about to continue the argument, but Antoni stayed firm. He led him to the door before urging him out and locking it behind him.

It was a fine balance. After what had happened last year, it would have been easy for Antoni to give in to fear and anxiety. Some days the struggle was worse than others, and he would have begged Roger for the chance to spend the night at his place rather than face it alone. This was not one of those days. Tonight, he felt stronger than he had in a long time.

There was one more thing he needed to do before he called it a night.

Dalton.

They hadn't seen each other since that morning, and he missed him. They had no plans to see each other that night, but Antoni needed to speak to him. It had been an exhausting day, and he stifled a yawn as he dialled

Dalton's number, but the second he answered, his spirit brightened.

"Hey. It's good to hear your voice," he said.

"You're not kidding," Dalton murmured, before letting out a weary sigh. "So, are you any wiser as to what's going on?"

"The police left about half an hour ago. They had nothing new to report. Are you all right?"

"Actually, yes. It sounds strange, right? But I feel okay. Absolutely knackered, but much better than yesterday. It's like things are finally progressing. I don't know how seriously the police are taking it, but they're looking at Catherine as a viable option. At least they think there's a connection between her disappearance and Larissa's death. That's better than nothing."

Antoni updated him on the CCTV footage the police had shown him from the neighbouring property.

"You're sure it's her?"

"Yes," he answered. "You would be, too, if you saw it. I've no doubt Justin will ID her, too. Anyone who knows her well enough will recognise her."

"I'm not sure Justin is ready to accept the truth. It means he's been played by my sister as much as the rest of us. The harsh reality won't be an easy thing for him to take."

A bruised ego is better than being dead, Antoni thought, but kept the notion to himself. There was little affection between Dalton and Catherine, but he doubted he wanted to hear her described as a killer. He might be thinking it, but it would be far worse to hear the words spoken aloud.

"Do you want me to come over?" Antoni asked. "Have you eaten yet?"

"I ordered a snack from room service. Listen… Don't take this the wrong way, but I'm beat. I'm already in bed and doubt I have the energy to last more than another ten minutes."

A tiny stab of rejection went through him, but he ignored it. Having argued with Roger to be left alone earlier, he knew how important it was to have time for yourself when things got rough. Sometimes sleep and quiet were the only things that worked.

"I understand. Get all the rest you need and call me if you change your mind. I'll be there in ten minutes, however late it is."

"You really are the greatest," Dalton said. "How about I treat you to breakfast instead? Come by the hotel early, say seven-thirty, and we'll have a couple of hours together before you go to work."

All thought of denial was banished. A quiet, restful night could be just what they both needed. "That's a date."

"I'm sure I don't need to tell you to make sure your place is well locked up tonight — until the police get an angle on Catherine's whereabouts."

"Already done. This place is locked up tighter than Fort Knox. Not even Goldfinger could get in."

They both chuckled then Dalton yawned loudly.

"Okay," Antoni said, "bedtime. Turn out the lights and try to get a good night's sleep. I'll see you in the morning."

"I can't wait. And, Antoni, thank you…for everything."

"There's no need."

"I know, but I have to say it anyway. I'm not sure I could have got through the last few days without you.

You've been a rock for me to cling to. I appreciate it so much."

The feeling of warmth spread all through him. Antoni blinked back the tears that pricked at his eyes. He wasn't going to cry over the phone. "I appreciate you, too. Now take care and sleep easy."

"Sleep well too, darling. I'll see you in the morning."

Chapter Twenty-One

Dalton thought the sound of his phone was the alarm. As he rolled across the bed on instinct, reaching out to shut off the noise, it took a few seconds to realise that the tone was different. The phone was ringing. The bedroom was in deep darkness. Through blurred vision, he saw the flashing handset on the side table and grabbed it. He stared at the screen, finding it almost impossible to focus. He blinked.

Justin, the display read.

What the hell is it now?

He ran his thumb across the green answer icon.

"Hello." He shuffled into a sitting position, rubbed his eyes and looked towards the hotel clock. 2:24, the digits read. Dalton had turned out the light at nine-thirty and had slept solidly until now, but he needed a lot more sleep than this. "What is it?"

His mind shifted through the reasons Justin could have to call him at this hour. Was he drunk and maudlin and needing someone to talk to? Or was he depressed and suffering insomnia as millions of possibilities ran through his mind.

"It's Catherine," Justin said.

What else?

"She wants to see us," Justin continued.

Dalton was instantly awake and turned on the bedside light. "What do you mean? You've heard from her?"

"She's in trouble. She needs our help."

He rubbed his eyes against the back of his arm, protecting them until they adjusted to the light. "What are you talking about? When did you speak to her?"

"Just now. Right before I called you."

"Where the hell is she? What did she say?"

"She said she needs to talk to us — in person, not over the phone." Justin's words tumbled out in a rush of nervous agitation. "Dalton, she's alive. She's safe. She wants us to come to her."

"Where is she?"

"She's going to text me the postcode. She doesn't want anyone else to know where she is yet, not after what happened to Larissa. Once we're on the road and almost there, she's going to let us know."

"Jesus, Justin. Do you realise how sketchy that sounds? You need to contact the police and let them find her."

"No," he shouted. "No police. If we involve them, she says she'll have to run again. The police can't help her. They will only make it worse."

Dalton groaned. *What the fuck has she got herself involved with now?* "What did she say about Larissa? Does she know who killed her?"

"Yes. She didn't tell me who. She said Larissa was caught up in it, too."

"*Caught up in* what?"

"I don't know." Justin sounded angry now. "But do you want Catherine to end up like her? That's why she's in hiding—because she'd be dead if anyone else knew where she was."

"Did she give you any idea what it's about? They are two social media influencers. It's not like they were drug dealers or running a people-trafficking ring. What could they be involved with that could get them killed?"

"Instead of asking me, why don't you wait and ask her? She wants us to go to her now…tonight. If you're so desperate to know what's going on, why don't you come with me and find out?"

"You're going to her? *Now*?"

"Yeah, but"—his tone softened—"I've been drinking. I don't want the cops to stop me when I'm on the way. It would ruin everything. I was hoping you would pick me up and we'd go together. Please, Dalton. She's your sister. She said she knows she's done things in the past to hurt you, but she needs you now."

"She could have called me herself if she wanted to convince me of that."

"She wants to see you in person. Isn't that more important—more genuine?"

Dalton sighed. This sounded like bullshit, but could he live with himself if any of it was true? If Catherine were in danger and he ignored her plea for help? She'd cried wolf so many times before, but what if this once she was genuine? "All right," he said at last. "I'll come on one condition."

"What?"

"When we find her, whatever she's mixed up in, we convince her to come with us to the police. If she's dug

202

herself into trouble, it won't do any good to keep on digging. We need to get her out of it."

Justin waited a long time before answering. "All right. I agree. I doubt she will, but we'll have to convince her together."

"Be ready in fifteen minutes."

Dalton got out of bed and hurried to the bathroom. He filled the basin with water and splashed it on his face. After everything he'd said in the last few days, all the suspicions he'd had about her, was he really going to head off blindly in the middle of the night to find her?

No fucking way.

Dalton couldn't be certain of even trusting Justin. There was nothing to say he wasn't involved in the whole mess. He'd even considered the possibility of him being behind it all. Larissa was dead, and there was no real evidence that Catherine was alive. Antoni was pretty sure the woman he'd seen in the alley was her, but he hadn't seen her face. There was no guarantee that any of this could be taken at face value.

He pulled on his clothes and tied his sneakers. This might be the stupidest thing he had ever done, but he would take out insurance. He removed his work mobile from his briefcase and turned it on. He hadn't used this device to contact Antoni and needed to copy over his number from his personal mobile phone. He composed a hasty message.

This is Dalton's work phone. I'm about to share my location with your device. Justin says he knows where Catherine is, and we're about to go there. Not sure it's a good idea, but if you haven't heard from me by seven in the morning, show this message to the police. Take care. I love you.

D xxx

He set up the location sharing function and hit send.

Dalton was certain that neither Justin nor Catherine was aware of his second phone. It was best that he kept it that way. He switched the device settings to silent and shoved it down his right sock and into his shoe. He would have to be conscious of his walking and not let it show, but better that minor discomfort than stumbling into a trap without protection.

If he suspected this was a trap, why was he even going?

Good question.

Because you might have done your sister a disservice – because she might really need you this time.

Fuck it. This was the closest he had come to the truth in days. He had to follow his instincts.

* * * *

The porch lights were on when he pulled onto Justin's drive. Moments later the front door opened, and Justin hurried out. He was dressed in dark jeans and a thick, padded jacket. The night was unseasonably cold and had taken Dalton by surprise. He had to spend several minutes warming the car and de-misting the windows before setting off from the hotel. Justin opened the passenger door and swung into the seat. The smell of alcohol wafted off him.

Not the best start.

"So, where are we going?" Dalton asked.

"Take the north road out of town. I'll tell you more on the way."

Dalton bit his lip and reversed off the drive. Anger and irritation flowed through his veins. He didn't know how long he'd be able to tolerate this mystery bullshit. The temptation to grab hold of Justin and wring the facts out of him was strong.

It was nearly three. The streets of Nyemouth were deserted, and they were out of town and heading north in a few minutes. Dalton gripped the wheel and focused on the roads. There were no streetlights to line the way, and he had to look ahead, alert to every curve and turn on the dark and unfamiliar roads.

"You said she's in trouble. Care to elaborate on that?" he asked.

"It will be better if Catherine tells you herself. That's why she asked to see you."

"You do realise how crazy this sounds? I don't even know why I'm humouring you on this."

Justin gave a loud huff. "It's only your sister, after all. Not like anyone important to you."

"*This*. This barmy scheme of driving through the night to find her? That's pure Catherine. That much I do believe. I just don't get why you're so keen to accommodate her mad plans. You realise this is exactly what she wants from you? To get you dancing to her tune. She's got you wrapped around her finger."

"Maybe it's because I love her, unlike her so-called family."

Dalton let that pass. Justin was besotted, so there was no point in trying to reason with him. "How much farther?"

"Stay on this road. Keep driving until I tell you to get off."

The route became more twisting as they progressed. *Where the hell is he taking me?* Dalton's suspicion that he was heading into a trap continued to bug him. Whenever he reached a rare straight stretch in the road, he risked a glance at Justin from the corner of his eye. In the light from the dashboard, the older man had a half smile on his face. Because he was going to see Catherine? Or because he was delivering Dalton to her.

Am I being paranoid? It was easy to think so, driving in the black of night to an unknown location.

"Can I have your phone?" Justin asked in a cold voice.

Dalton tensed, alert. "Why?"

"Catherine says we need to turn them off, so we can't be followed." He held out his hand. "Give it to me. I'll do it while you concentrate on driving."

Dalton's mouth was paper dry. "That's a bit extreme, don't you think?" He heard the note of panic in his tone.

"Those are her rules. Come on. Hand it over. I'm not going to chuck it out of the window, you know. I just want to turn it off so we can't be traced. Look." He raised his own device and pressed the off switch. The screen illuminated before fading to black. Justin held out his hand.

Dalton knew he was safe, that he had the secret phone to fall back on, but decided to play along, just to learn how desperate Justin was. "I thought you said she was going to send you her location. How can she do that with a dead phone?"

Justin sighed. "All right, you've got me. She already did that." He tapped his forehead. "And it's stored in here. Now give me your phone. We don't need them, and they could compromise Catherine."

"*Compromise*? You make it sound like she's in witness protection or something." Dalton let out a false laugh, pretending to make light of the situation.

He glanced sideways and found Justin staring directly at him. After a moment he said, "Who's to say she's not? Now, give me the phone or I can't tell you where to find her. That's the rules."

"But I thought she wanted to see us. Isn't that what we're doing here, driving to the middle of nowhere?"

"All right, smart arse, that's enough. Just give me your fucking phone. *Now*."

Fuck. He's as unhinged as she is. Dalton realised what a terrible mistake he had made. He braked gradually and pulled the car over to the side of the road.

"No. This stops here. I'm turning the car around, and we're going to the police. Then you'll tell them everything you know."

Justin's hand shot forward and wrapped around his throat, squeezing hard. The pressure threatened to crush his windpipe. Dalton grasped at his hand, trying to worm his fingers around it. It was impossible to breathe as he choked. Justin's face was right beside his in the dull light.

"That's not the way this is going to work." Justin's voice came through gritted teeth. "I thought you might bitch like this and try to turn around. Here's something for you to think about. Larissa is not the only one who could find themselves washed up along the coast. Your little fuck-boy Antoni? He had a lucky escape last year. He might not be so fortunate a second time. What's to say he won't float in on the tide in a day or two with a stab wound in his chest? Now wouldn't that be a shame?"

Justin loosened his grip a fraction, allowing Dalton to take a breath.

Antoni. What had he gotten him involved with? His beautiful, talented boyfriend, who had already been through hell... How could he put him at further risk?

He stretched his neck, struggling to speak. Justin eased the pressure a little more.

"If I do what you want, you'll leave him alone?"

"I don't see that you're in a position to make bargains, but he's safe enough for now...*if* you do what the fuck you're told."

Tears blurred his vision. Hopelessly, Dalton nodded.

"Isn't that better?" Justin said, letting go of his neck. "Give me your damn phone."

Dalton reached into his jacket and handed over his personal device. Justin waved it aside.

"Turn it off first."

Dalton did as he was told before passing it to Justin. Justin opened the passenger window and tossed it out. Dalton prayed he wasn't bright enough to search him for the second device. It could be hours before Antoni woke up and saw the message, but whatever happened, he hoped it would be enough to guide the police to his whereabouts. He might be dead by then, but his text to Antoni would at least point the finger at Justin.

"Now fucking *drive*," Justin said. "Stay on this road."

Dalton did as he was told, fighting to keep his calm. He couldn't lose it to anger or panic. He'd need all his wits to survive whatever happened next.

"Are we really going to see Catherine? Or is she dead, too? Just like Larissa."

Justin scoffed. "You really are a crafty shit. You think you're always one step ahead, don't you?"

"Unlike you, you mean. Who's been playing us for fools since Saturday morning. You're a good actor. I'll give you that much. You had me convinced for most of the time."

"It wasn't difficult. Catherine told me all about you before you arrived. She told me what strings to pull to make you dance." He sniggered.

What the hell is this? Has he killed Catherine and Larissa? Or is Catherine behind it all?

Either way, Dalton couldn't work out a strong enough motive for either version. One person was dead. That was a fact. Catherine had always been a narcissist—deluded, but psychopathic?

The swimming pool. Remember? Hadn't she tried to kill him when he was a kid?

"I don't believe you're up to this," Dalton said, glancing at Justin. "A self-made businessman suddenly flips and risks it all by going on a murderous rampage? Nah. No chance. It's Catherine for sure. What did she promise you? What could she offer that would make you do this? Are you that pussy-struck?"

"Keep your mind on the fucking driving," Justin snarled, "unless you want my hands around your throat again. And don't forget Antoni still isn't in the clear."

"That answers my question," Dalton said with false bravado. "I obviously touched a nerve. You're just my sister's bitch. You know it as well as I do."

Justin's fist flew across the car, striking him on the arm. Dalton let go of the wheel. The vehicle swerved onto the other side of the road, before he wrestled it back under control. Despite the pain, it gave him a small advantage. Justin was acting on Catherine's orders. He was obviously obsessed with her. Dalton could use that against him. He just didn't know how yet.

"Watch out for a right turning," Justin said, gesturing at the road ahead. "Should be coming up soon."

Dalton reduced his speed and half a mile later he saw a sign for the turn. The smaller road was narrower and more twisting than the first, and he had to keep to under thirty miles an hour to navigate its dangerous bends in the absolute darkness. They were climbing, driving upwards on the moors.

After another four miles, Justin said, "There'll be a turning on the left soon. It's not sign posted. You'll need to look out for it."

Dalton followed his direction, and they were no longer on any established road, just a barren dirt track, covered in deep potholes. He kept his speed to under twenty and steered carefully around them. The car shuddered and jolted, and he feared he had done permanent damage when something scraped against the underside. He slowed to ten miles per hour and kept going, always moving upwards.

His heart seemed to beat in his throat.

They were reaching the end.

Catherine had hidden herself away in the middle of nowhere, but soon the mystery would be over and they would come face-to-face again.

He checked the clock on the dashboard. Ten to four. They were only about a fifty-minute drive north of Nyemouth. She hadn't even gone that far — far enough to hide, but close enough to watch her scheme unfold.

The pounding in Dalton's head intensified. He took more deep breaths. *Got to keep it together.*

As he rounded another bend, he detected a faint glow in the distance. Coming closer, he saw there was a house ahead—a two-storey building, out on the moors, all alone. *The perfect hideaway.*

"Around to the side," Justin directed.

He pulled onto a wide courtyard. From what he could make out, it was an old farmhouse. A separate barn ran behind the main property. There were boarded windows, and the roof was in a state of dilapidation. The concrete of the driveway was cracked and overgrown with weeds, while a low stone wall ran around the perimeter. The farm had long since been abandoned.

Justin opened the side door, activating the interior light of the car. For the first time, Dalton saw the look of glee on his face.

"C'mon," he gloated. "What are you waiting for? It's time for the family reunion. This is what you came for, isn't it?"

Dalton swallowed. *Stay strong. Get them talking. You only have to keep them here long enough for Antoni to alert the police. Hold out until morning, and this could all be over.*

He got out of the car and took a sharp breath. The temperature up here must be several degrees cooler than in town.

There was a dull glow of light from what he assumed must be the kitchen of the house. It shifted and moved, suggesting candles. Had Catherine been holed up here for days with no electricity?

The back door opened. Dalton froze. Justin came around the car to stand beside him.

"This is the part I've been waiting for," he whispered to Dalton.

There she was. She raised a lantern with a thick pillar candle inside. Its flickering amber glow softened her sharp features. She was dressed in black, jeans and a winter jacket, with her hair hidden beneath a woollen cap—a world away from the glamorous image she projected online.

She came out of the house and walked towards them.

Dalton flashed back to that incident in the pool, the day she had tried to kill him, and he saw the same expression on her face now—the triumphant glitter in her eyes.

She reached into her pocket and produced a black handgun.

"Oh, my God," he cried. "You can't be serious. Is this what it's come to?"

She gave a gloating smile and shrugged. "It's what we've always been leading to, little brother." She raised the gun and pointed it at his face. She stood less than six feet away from him.

Fuck. She's nuts.

There was no chance of making it until morning. No rescue from Antoni. He would never see his sweet, beautiful boyfriend again.

Catherine's thin lips split into a reptilian grin. She levelled the gun.

Dalton forced his eyes to stay open. She would have to look into them before she killed him.

"Goodbye, sweetie," she said.

At the last second, Catherine pivoted and fired.

The sound was deafening, followed by the hot splash of something wet against his face.

Dalton raised his hands instinctively and turned as Justin crashed backwards to the floor. His face was unrecognisable. She had shot her lover in the head.

As Dalton's ears adjusted to the noise of the shot, he heard the gleeful laughter of his sister.

Chapter Twenty-Two

Dalton stared at the body on the ground—the bloody mess that used to be Justin. His brain ran at a reduced capacity, struggling to deal with what had happened and unable to focus on the present. For a few seconds, he tried to convince himself this was just a game—a carefully staged act between Catherine and Justin to fuck with him, an illusion of props and make-up. But as his faculties returned, he only had to look at the mess on the concrete drive to know it was for real.

Unable to comprehend, he turned to Catherine.

She held the lantern in front of her, throwing light on the corpse of her boyfriend, as though admiring her work.

"He loved you." The words fell from his mouth, though he had no awareness of saying them.

Catherine smirked. "Of course he did. They all love me...everyone except you. You know, it's been quite hurtful to hear some of the stuff you've been saying since I disappeared, that my own flesh and blood had

214

zero concern for my welfare. It's almost like you didn't care. You know what, baby brother? That hurt." Her words dripped with sarcasm.

Her callous detachment brought Dalton's back to the present. "It would appear my instincts were correct."

"Not good enough, though, were they? If you had any real sense, you would have fucked off back to the family ranch instead of ending up here, exactly where I want you."

"What… What the hell are you doing?"

The smile dropped, and her face hardened. "Later. It's fucking freezing out here. Get in the car."

He stared at her incredulously. "Why?"

She raised the gun. "Unless you want your pretty face to end up like a smashed watermelon, just like old Justin here, do what the fuck you're told. Now *move*."

She stepped around to the other side of the car, keeping the weapon trained on him the whole time. Dalton considered his options, and for now, there were none. She'd already proven what a good shot she was and that she had no problem with pulling the trigger. One wrong move and she would finish him.

He moved to the car. He still had the keys. His thighs trembled as he walked, stepping around the pool of blood that surged from Justin's body. The only comfort he took was in the reassuring presence of the phone pressed against his ankle. He climbed into the driver's seat. Catherine slid in from the other side, the weapon trained on his head.

Where did she get the gun from? And how does she know how to use it? Catherine was far more dangerous than he'd ever given her credit for.

"Where are we going?" he asked.

"Over there." She pointed towards the derelict barn. The front gates were open. "Move the car inside."

There was no point in questioning the motives of a crazy woman. Dalton started the engine and did as she'd asked, steering into the building. The interior was empty. Any farming equipment that might have been there had long been stripped away. Once inside, he braked.

"Now what?"

"Turn off the engine and get out."

There was no natural light. The only illumination came from Catherine's flickering lantern. Dalton got out of the car. He had no choice. If he tried to fight her for the gun, she would pull the trigger before he got close. In the tiny chance he could take it from her, what would he do with it? He had never fired a gun in his life. This was not the time to start.

Something scuttled away in the darkness to his right. *Rats, no doubt.* He shuddered. How bizarre that he should fear a small animal when his own sister had just proven she was a killer.

Not just a killer, but a psychopath.

Holding the lantern high, she looked like a mad woman from a gothic novel. She grinned again. In the ghoulish light of the candle, she had never seemed more evil. She was no mad woman. She was a witch.

"Are you scared?" she asked, little more than a whisper.

"That's your intention, isn't it?" He hated the quivering pitch of his voice.

"As a matter of fact, it is." She snorted. "It was my favourite hobby when I was young—making my bratty brothers snivel and cry. Easy, too. You were soft, the pair of you—wrapped in cotton wool from the minute you were born. You were incapable of withstanding the slightest push. Are you going to cry for me again, Dalton? Just like you used to as a shitty kid."

The more she talked, the calmer he became. This was the Catherine he was used to, the bully he'd grown up with. The sophisticated woman she had presented at the party on Friday had been an act...a poor masquerade. Tonight, he'd been reunited with his real sister, the spiteful, manipulative bitch who had blighted his childhood.

Keep her talking. The longer he drew out whatever she had planned, the closer he would be to morning and the faint hope that the police would trace him here.

"I was never that scared of you," he lied. "I looked up to you, you know. Why wouldn't I? I was a baby, and you were my big sister. You were the cool one, doing all the things we weren't allowed to."

She cackled. "Oh, nice try. You really are the idiot I took you for. Do you think I'm going to fall for false flattery now? I have planned and plotted this every step of the way. You're here because I want you to be. I've played you better than a fiddle." Another laugh. "I won't deny it's been fun, though." She gestured with the gun. "Back outside."

He could barely see a step in front of him, the darkness was so complete, until Catherine came up behind him and illuminated the way ahead.

"Into the house," she said.

The eerie Halloween glow of her lantern cast light over the brutal remains of Justin.

"What about him?" Dalton asked. "Was he part of the plan?"

Her voice was cold. "He was easier to manipulate than you were. All men fall somewhere on the scale of stupidity. It's just a case of figuring out where they are and reeling them in accordingly."

"And killing him? Was that always your intention?"

"Of course it was. You don't think I could suffer a fool like that to live. Finally getting to kill him was just a bonus. It's a shame I can't share just how badass I am with my followers. Imagine how many likes I'd get if I'd recorded his execution."

The fact his sister could make light of the murder she had just committed sickened and terrified him. He had always considered her to be emotionally deficient, but her lack of remorse or empathy was horrifying.

"C'mon. Get the fuck inside. I'm freezing my arse off here."

She let out a high, mocking laugh.

Dalton wondered how close they were to the dawn.

* * * *

Antoni rolled over in bed and looked at the illuminated digits of his alarm clock, seven minutes past four. He had gone to bed at eleven. That was almost five hours of continuous, uninterrupted sleep…a new personal best. He turned and stretched, pressing his body into the cool, far reaches of the bed. After spending several nights with Dalton, it was strange to sleep alone again. Not that he should get used to Dalton being around… He had avoided dwelling on the subject, but they would soon have to face the fact that Dalton would be leaving Nyemouth.

But not yet. Antoni pushed the thought away.

He was wide awake, and his bladder wouldn't let him sleep again until he relieved it. He pulled back the covers and got out of bed. The chill hit him instantly, and he grabbed his robe from the back of the chair and pulled it on. He didn't turn on the lights. He could find his way well enough in the dark, and light might banish any potential he had to fall back asleep.

Stumbling to the bathroom with half-closed eyes, he lifted the seat and released the stream.

If it hadn't been for the urge to urinate, he wondered how much longer he would have slept for. It was usually the nightmares that tore him from slumber, but not tonight. He couldn't remember having any bad dreams at all.

They had reduced in frequency of late but hadn't left him altogether. Most nights he relived some of his encounter with the man with the knife. Antoni doubted he would ever be gone for good.

He flushed and washed his hands.

Wandering back to the bedroom, barefooted, he realised just how low the temperature had gotten. The summer months and balmy nights were still some weeks away. By the time he slipped off his robe and got back beneath the covers, he was wide awake. *Bugger.* He shouldn't complain, not after sleeping for so long already.

He gazed at the shadowy patterns on the ceiling and thought about Dalton. It wasn't that long until their breakfast date. Maybe he would get up and get dressed soon. He could go out with his camera and capture some shots of the dawn breaking over the harbour before meeting Dalton at Quay House. He wondered if today would be the day they would have to face the inevitable and discuss the practicalities of Dalton leaving. There was no doubt they would keep in touch. Antoni was sure of that. But what kind of relationship would they have from opposite ends of the country, with Dalton in the south and him here in the north? Video calls and occasional weekend visits would not be enough to keep the magic alive.

He turned over again and after a few more minutes returned his gaze to the clock. *Four-fifteen.*

Fuck it.

There was no point in wasting time like this. He reached across and turned on the bedside lamp. He would read until five, and if he still wasn't tired, he'd get up. His mobile phone sat on top of the novel he'd been half-heartedly reading for a couple of weeks. Out of habit he snatched the phone first to see if he had any messages.

There was one from an unknown number.

When he realised it was from Dalton and understood what it said, he swung to the edge of the bed, instantly alert. He tapped the link to access the phone tracker.

What? Where the hell?

Dalton was at some place in the arse end of nowhere, around forty miles north of here.

Why was he meeting Catherine in the middle of the night? And in such a remote spot.

If you haven't heard from me by seven in the morning, show this message to the police.

That didn't sound good. What was he even thinking going up there after all the things he'd said about Catherine and his suspicions of what had happened to Larissa?

A massive warning sign went off in Antoni's head. The same feeling of dread and inevitability he'd experienced in the seconds before he was stabbed in the stomach.

This is all wrong.

He hurried to the wardrobe and started pulling out clothes. There was no way he could wait until seven. Dalton could be in all kinds of trouble with that twisted sister of his.

He was going up there *now*.

Chapter Twenty-Three

Dalton entered the kitchen ahead of Catherine. A fire burned in the hearth, though it did little to warm the room, which was thick with the sour smell of damp and decay. There were more candles and lanterns lit about the place. Most of the kitchen units were missing doors and drawers. The floor was comprised of cracked and uneven terracotta tiles. It appeared to have been abandoned for at least the last twenty years.

He spotted a half-eaten loaf of bread on the countertop, some food cartons and dozens of empty wine bottles.

"This is where you've been hiding?" he asked incredulously.

"It would hardly have been inconspicuous if I checked into a five-star hotel with room service," she scoffed. "I knew no one would ever look for me here, and I was right."

"What the hell for?"

"Never mind all that. Start touching things."

What fresh madness is this? "What?"

Catherine had put down the lantern and now brandished the gun in both hands. "You're not fucking deaf. Do as I say. Start touching shit. C'mon. The door handles, the tabletop, the kitchen counter. I want your fingerprints all over this place."

He stood there, staring at her in complete shock. She was deranged. He could hear it in the cracked pitch of her voice, see it in the flashing whites of her eyes down the barrel of the handgun.

"Just because Justin is dead, it doesn't mean your little fancy-man is safe. Now do what I fucking tell you, or one of these bullets will find its way into Antoni's skull. I think I've already proven how good my aim is. I could finish Antoni before he even knows I'm there."

He did as she'd asked and moved around the kitchen, laying his fingers on the grubby Formica surface of the table, touching the food cartons and work tops.

"I must admit I didn't see that coming," she said. It was the condescending tone she used to use when they were kids. The big, disgruntled sister taking her anger out on her younger brother. "You hooking up with Antoni. It took me quite by surprise. I mean, he's cute enough, good-looking if you like that kind of thing, but I've always found him really boring. But then, I hadn't been keeping tabs on you for long. I had no idea of the kind of men you were into. If I'd known you were going to fall so hard and fast, I might have arranged for him to take a dip in the sea the other night instead of Larissa."

He maintained his composure. Refusing to provide the reaction she wanted. "Why her? You were friends, weren't you? Why did you have to kill Larissa?"

"Why not?" Catherine chuckled. It was a cold, emotionless sound. "Besides, I didn't kill her. *You* did."

"You'll never convince anyone of that. It's a crazy idea."

"Don't you worry about that, Dalton. I'm very persuasive when I need to be. By the time I'm finished here and done with you, I'll have amassed a nice pile of evidence against you. I've even got the hammer you used to kill poor Larissa. I'll be getting your prints all over that baby soon enough. Larissa, Justin... You've been on quite a killing spree, as well as the kidnap and torture of your only sister."

She really thinks she can get away with this. He had to be very careful. She was clearly insane or evil...or both. She had killed two people already and hadn't displayed a hint of remorse. How long had he been here now? Were they any closer to being discovered?

Like a megalomaniac villain in a Bond movie, she relished the chance to prove how clever she had been. *Keep her talking. Let's discover the full extent of her scheme.*

"So that's it. You're going to pretend *I've* been holding you captive here all this time?"

She licked her lips and nodded. "Beautiful, isn't it? My little brother, who has always been jealous of my lifestyle and success, goes completely crazy and kidnaps me. Only that's not enough... He has to go further and murder both of my lovers." She laughed. "Can you imagine what the tabloids are going to make of that? They'll eat it up. All my followers will be just gagging to hear the details of my ordeal with my psycho sibling. There'll be TV and magazine interviews, giving my side of the story. Book deals, podcasts, hell, why not a Netflix docuseries recounting the whole tragic mess? It will be must-see television, don't you think?"

None of this crazy talk would ever add up. No matter how cunning she thought she had been or how she'd tried to seed the false evidence, she would never pin this story on him. There were witnesses, and security cameras that would place him in Nyemouth in the days she'd been missing. He had barely left the centre of town. Quay House had cameras in all the corridors that would place him there for most of the time…if anyone cared to look. Was she wily enough to convince the police of what she said? Enough to stop their investigation? Unlikely, especially once their parents got involved. His mother would see straight through Catherine's lies.

There was no need to point that out now. Let her revel in her glory.

"How long have you been planning this?"

She shrugged. "A while. I had the idea several years ago, in fact. It was kind of vague. I knew what I wanted to do but not *how* to do it. It was only when I came to Nyemouth and met Justin, then found this place, that I could finally see a way to make it happen. The place and time were perfect, and I could at last see a way to make my dreams come true."

He took in the grimy kitchen, slowly digesting what she had said. "Why?" he said at last. "Do you really hate me that much?"

"Of course I do. Do you think you're here because I fucking *like* you? Jesus. Deluded much? I hate all of you — the whole fucking family — but you're the golden boy, the one our bitch mother adores the most. That's what will make this so special. Your death will cut that cunt to the core. I can't see that she'll ever get over it.

And the scandal that follows? Discovering what a twisted little fuck her baby boy was all along... That's going to be so delightful. I'm almost certain it will kill the bitch. She won't be able to take it... But not too soon. I want her to stew in misery and feel bad in ways she never thought possible."

"Jesus, Catherine. What has brought you to this? How can you be so full of hate? Our family always tried to do the best for you and get you the help you needed. You threw everything back and lashed out whenever someone tried to help you."

"What the hell do you know? You were just a kid. You weren't around for most of it."

"I was there when you tried to kill me. The swimming pool in Spain."

Her eyes widened in genuine surprise. "You remember that? I thought you were too young."

"I remember," he said, exasperated.

"I'm glad," she said. "And I'm glad you told me, because I failed in this task once before. I sure as shit won't fail again."

* * * *

Antoni headed north, following the tracker on Dalton's phone. His knuckles showed white against the steering wheel as he peered into the darkness ahead. He was twenty-three miles from his destination. Dalton hadn't moved since he'd begun the journey. His own phone was linked to his car Bluetooth. He hit the redial option for the police and listened to the automated voice options. He hissed in frustration as he waited for the connection.

"It's Antoni Nowak again," he said in a rush when the operator answered. "I called about ten minutes ago. I'm trying to get in touch with DS Norton or DS Williams. Have you managed to track either of them down yet?"

"Do you have the collar numbers for those officers?" the operator asked.

Damn it.

"No. I explained all that before. It's important that I speak to them or anyone else who might be involved in the investigation into Catherine Caine's disappearance or the murder of Larissa Crawford."

"Do you have information relating to the investigation?" the man on the phone asked cautiously.

"Yes," he snapped. "I've already been through this. I think I know where you can find Catherine Caine." He reeled off the location information from Dalton's phone. "Like I said last time, I'm on my way now. You need to get some officers out there *fast.*"

"What makes you think she is in that area?"

Antoni struggled to keep calm. He wanted to shout and rage down the phone. No one understood the urgency of the situation.

"I've had a message from Dalton Caine, Catherine's brother. He was on his way to meet her there, but I've had no further contact from him since. After what happened to Larissa, I think he's in danger."

"What kind of danger?"

Oh my God. "Can you ask me all these questions later? Just get someone out there to find them. I'm on my way, and I'll tell your officers all they want to know. But please *hurry.*"

"We currently don't have any officers in that area. I will send out the first available response unit."

Antoni swore and hung up so he could give his full attention to the road. He didn't want to miss an instruction or turn off. Likely he would be the first person on the scene. The cops were investigating a murder, but they didn't seem to be taking his information seriously.

He'd already tried calling Dalton's regular phone, which had gone straight to voicemail. He hadn't tried the second device. He suspected Dalton wouldn't want Catherine to know about it, and he couldn't take a chance on giving him away.

He couldn't stop thinking about Dalton's story of the day his sister had tried to kill him. Dalton thought Catherine was capable of anything – and now, so did he.

Dalton's text said Justin was taking him there. Was Justin involved too, or was he another victim of the con? Antoni had no choice. Prepare for the worst and assume the two of them were in it together.

He had rushed off unprepared. What did he have in the car that he could use as a weapon if it came to that? *Not much.* He wracked his brain, trying to remember what was in the boot. *A can of antifreeze that might even be close to empty.* Still, it would work at close range if he got one of them in the eyes or mouth. *What else? Think.* Last autumn he had bought an emergency snow shovel ready for winter. It was heavy duty steel that folded down to a compact size for storage. It would make another effective weapon, but only at very close range.

They were better than nothing.

The greatest weapon he had was surprise. No one knew Dalton had informed him of their location. He'd have to hope he could get there without being seen or heard.

There was a right-hand turn coming up. Antoni reduced his speed and came off the main road, heading onto the moors. His knowledge of the area was vague. Even in daylight he would struggle to find his way around these twisting roads. He nudged the speed back up to fifty. It was dangerous with all these sudden and unexpected bends, but he couldn't delay a second longer than necessary.

Dalton's life depended on him.

Antoni was certain of that.

* * * *

Dalton noticed a wooden chair in the corner of the kitchen. There were two lengths of rope wrapped around the sturdy arms and a ratty looking cushion on the seat.

"What's that for?" he asked. It was pitch black beyond the dirty windows and dawn was still some way off. He had to keep stalling for time. "Are you going to tie me up?"

"Of course not." Her voice tickled with amusement. "It would be something of a giveaway if they found you with rope burns on your wrists. No, brother. That's where you tied *me* up." She raised an arm and shook down the sleeve of her jacket, revealing the red chafe marks on her skin. "See? I had to put up quite a struggle to get free."

She might be mad, but she had thought it all through. He tried a different track. "Please, Catherine, come on. It doesn't have to be like this. You don't have to fight everything and everyone. You could let us in. Let *me* in. We can get you the help you need."

Her voice hardened. "If you're talking about the kind of help our fucking mother got for me as a kid, forget it. All those whack-job doctors did was train me how to better hide what I was really feeling. The more questions they asked, the more skilled I got at lying and telling them what they wanted to hear. That's what most people want, after all. Justin, Larissa, even you. Just bait the trap with the right words and watch them get tangled up."

Dalton cast his mind back to childhood and the strange fascination he'd had whenever Catherine had gone off for one of her special appointments — the ones his parents wouldn't talk about, the times when he and Tobias were told to mind their own business. Tobias, being a couple of years older, had been the first to guess what was going on. They used to whisper about it when they played in their treehouse and garden dens, careful not to let the adults overhear them.

Catherine had been even more sullen and uncommunicative when she came back from one of her trips to the psychiatrist. It was only later, when he was older and having a difficult spell at university, that he understood some of what she must have gone through. As his own counsellor forced him to confront the issues buried deep in his past, Dalton developed an understanding and, at last, sympathy for his sister.

For what? Absolutely nothing. The doctors hadn't made her better. They had only made her more cunning and dangerous.

"It doesn't mean it won't work now," he said, helplessly. He didn't believe it any more than she would, but it was the only way he had to keep her engaged. "You can still have a family. It's not too late."

"Christ. You're really not too bright. What part of I-hate-every-fucking-one-of-you don't you understand? Eh? I don't want to be part of your damn family. I want to destroy it. And I'm starting right now, with you."

Fuck. Her crazy expression had intensified. *This is it.* He had run out of options. He couldn't save himself, but he hoped he'd done enough in alerting Antoni, to bring the police here and let them uncover the truth.

"You must have realised by now that I have a very detailed plan," she continued. "I'm going to destroy every one of them. You are first and our mother last, because I want her to hurt more than any of you other fuckers. And for that, you must die."

She raised the gun in a two-handed grip and levelled it at his head.

His insides were liquid with fear, but he wouldn't let her see it. "Do your worst. You can kill me, but you won't get away with it. I'm sure of that." He returned her crazy smile with of his own. "You're really not as clever as you think you are."

Her expression froze. Dalton thought his last comments had gotten through to her. He'd done it. He'd rattled her. Then her saw her eyes tilt towards the door and her head shifted, listening.

It was difficult to hear because of the pounding in his own head. He strained and heard nothing but the empty isolation of the moors. Catherine became even more intent.

Then he heard it. The sound of an engine in the night — someway distant but coming closer.

The police? Had Antoni done it? Had he alerted the cops?

"You might as well give in now," Dalton said. "It's over. I've had a tracker on me the whole time."

A visible darkness passed across her face and a sudden chill skittered down Dalton's spine. In that moment, he realised he had just had a glimpse of raw, undiluted evil.

Catherine was in a daze — only for a second, then she snapped out of it. She raised the gun again.

"It looks like my plan will have to be adapted."

Chapter Twenty-Four

The road conditions worsened as Antoni drove higher onto the moors, navigating the sudden bends and turns. He hadn't passed a building or another vehicle for miles. This was truly the middle of nowhere. If Catherine had been hiding out here, it was no surprise she hadn't been found. And the dark was absolute. He couldn't see a thing beyond the range of his headlights.

He had to find something soon. The phone locator showed that Dalton was now less than a mile and a half away, but as he drove farther, the distance suddenly grew greater again. Dalton was now two miles away. Antoni brought the car to a stop at the side of the road, staring at the screen. It was true, he was moving away. He must have missed a turn somewhere back there.

Shit.

Fighting to control his deepening unease, he performed a careful U-turn and headed back the way he had come, keeping his speed to fifteen miles per hour so he could watch for any signs. There was a dirty track ahead of him. He slowed to a stop again.

There was nothing to indicate where the road led, but that had to be it. There was nowhere else to go. He rechecked his phone screen. Dalton was located a little over a mile away to the right. Antoni gazed into the darkness. There was nothing there but black, empty space.

He drummed his hands on the wheel, his heart hammering against his ribs.

"Fuck it."

He got out of the car and opened the boot, pulling out the snow shovel and the can of antifreeze. He gave it a shake. *Half full. Perfect.* He hunted around for anything else he could use as a weapon but there was nothing other than a blanket. These would have to do. Getting back in the front, he threw the items into the footwell of the passenger seat and released the handbrake.

"I'm coming for you," he muttered, and hoped it wouldn't be too late.

He took the right-hand turn and followed the rugged track.

* * * *

"Out the back," Catherine said, jerking the gun towards the door.

"You might as well give up," Dalton continued to plead. "You can't get away now."

"And still, he underestimates me. *Out,*" she shouted.

She kept her distance as Dalton moved towards the door. There was no chance of him tackling her or knocking the gun from her grip. He knew better than to try it. Catherine would shoot without hesitation if he made any unexpected move. His only chance was to let her think she had the upper hand and hope an opportunity, anything, would present itself.

The phone rubbed against his ankle as he walked. He did his best to maintain an even pace and avoid drawing attention to it. He hoped the car they could hear was the police, but if not, the phone would still be useful. If Catherine asked for the tracking device, he would lie and tell her it was in his watch.

The handle was stiff and rusty, and it took some effort to shake and rattle it loose until the door opened.

"Straight out," Caroline directed. "Round the front to the road so we can see who's coming. And don't get any stupid ideas or I'll blow your spine out."

She had left the lantern inside, and the night was so dark that his eyes couldn't adjust.

Dalton stumbled forward, his hands splayed in front of him.

He saw a set of headlights winding their way up the hill.

There was no relief. This could be the most dangerous moment yet. Catherine had no clue what was happening. Her careful plot was going off script, and she would be at her most alert. He wondered just how twitchy her finger was on that trigger.

"Keep walking forward," she told him. "Hands up...out into the road. That's it."

Each step was more uncertain than the last. The concrete courtyard was cracked and uneven, but when he came onto the rutted track, the route was even more treacherous. He stepped into a pothole and jarred his ankle, hissing as a bolt of pain shot through him.

"Keep moving," Catherine barked.

The headlights were closer now. Dalton prickled with unease. No sign of blue lights. Was this even a police car? Just a regular vehicle? The realisation hit like a truck. *Antoni. No.* He had followed the tracker himself rather than alert the cops. Panicking, he spun around, hoping to make a desperate lunge for Catherine.

She was too far away. He made out her figure in the dark, the gun held in both hands, her stance wide and steady.

The noise of the car grew closer. Suddenly it was behind him, and Catherine was illuminated in its headlights. She was possessed by all the rage, spite and hatred that had festered in her since childhood.

"Don't," Dalton cried, waving his arms, hoping he would take the bullet rather than Antoni.

She fired. Once. Twice.

Both bullets whizzed past him.

Dalton was never their target.

He spun around as he heard the impact with the car. The windscreen fragmented. A vicious screech of rubber and metal tore across the silence of the moors. The vehicle veered violently to the left, and he watched in horror as it went off the road. The front end crumpled as it ploughed into a ditch, impacting with a tree.

Dalton rushed forward.

"Stay where the fuck you are," Catherine screamed, "unless you want your head blown apart right where you stand."

Dalton hesitated. Every instinct impelled him towards the vehicle and to Antoni, but Catherine wasn't kidding. She would gun him down before he got close. He looked over at the wreck. No sign of movement. But there was a chance, surely, that Antoni was alive. The car couldn't have been travelling that fast, not on these roads. With a seat belt and airbag, he could have survived.

If her bullets didn't kill him first.

He couldn't think like that. *Have hope. Antoni has lived through worse things than my mad sister.*

He still had the phone. He prayed that Antoni had contacted the police before setting out on this risky mission, but if not, it was up to him to make that call. Somehow, he would have to find a way.

My best chance is to keep her away from the car. If she finds he's alive, she'll shoot him.

He turned to face her with his hands raised.

Catherine now held the gun in one hand. In the other, she had her own mobile phone and had activated the flashlight function. Her mouth was open, taking quick, ragged breaths. She watched him and let out a short, uncertain laugh. "They always blow up in the movies."

Jesus. Whenever he thought he'd reached his capacity for horror, she managed to take it further. "You're a monster," he said quietly, more to himself than to her.

"This can still work," she said, ignoring him. Then louder, with more conviction, "It can still work."

"Forget it. Whatever you thought you were doing, it's over. Can't you see that? Can't you get it into your thick head?"

"No, brother. Unlike you, I don't settle. I make situations work for me. This is just a blip. I'll still make it look like it's all your fault. Now come on, *move.* We're getting out of here."

"Where the hell to?"

"I'll think of that on the way. Now c'mon. Back to your car." She jerked her gun hand towards the barn.

Just do as she says for now. She was at sea, her plans scuppered. An opportunity to overpower her and take the weapon could still present itself. With his hands raised, the model of docile compliancy, he did as she'd asked. The light from her phone made the return trip across the courtyard easier than before, keeping clear of the prone corpse on the ground.

The barn was eerily quiet. Even the rats had ceased scuttling in the dark corners.

"Have you got the keys?" she asked, still behind him, keeping a cautious distance.

Dalton patted himself. They were in his right trouser pocket, but he searched everywhere else first, casting furtive glances around the barn, hoping to find something, anything, he could use as a weapon. It was too damn dark to see beyond the minor range of her phone light. "I've got them," he said at last.

"Get in," she said. "Driver's seat."

He unlocked the car and slipped into the front. Catherine walked around the vehicle and climbed into the rear passenger seat. *Damn.* If she'd got in the front, at close quarters, he might have stood a chance of getting the gun—or surprising her the second her concentration faltered.

"Let's go," she said.

"Where?"

"Just get out of here, you bastard. I'll tell you where once we're on the way."

She was operating blind, without a plan. It was clear in the jittering pitch of her voice.

Dalton fastened his seat belt and pressed the ignition.

"This can still work," Catherine said. "This can still work." She repeated the words like a mantra.

* * * *

The airbag had deployed on impact, saving Antoni from the worst of the crash. He sat in his seat, catching his breath as the safety device deflated. There was pain in his right shoulder from where he'd been thrown forward against the seat belt. His collarbone might have been broken. He moved his head slowly from side to side and experienced no other pain than a pounding headache. Cautiously, he tested his extremities—his legs, arms—and nothing seemed to be broken there.

The windscreen was gone. It had shattered when the first bullet struck and disintegrated completely when the car had come off the road.

Catherine. He had seen her just for a moment in the headlights, standing behind Dalton, taking aim. She'd fired at the car twice, and now she was with Dalton.

Antoni released the seat belt. Fresh pain burned through his shoulder at the sudden movement. There was something broken there. It was minor. He would live. His priority was to make sure Dalton survived his psycho sister.

His phone had been thrown loose from its holder in the crash. He leaned forward to search the footwell and was struck by a searing pain in his chest. He gasped and sat back, taking short, agonising breaths. *Fuck.* Something was broken inside—at least one rib. There was a metallic taste in his mouth. *Blood.*

You're still alive, he reminded himself. *And no stranger to pain.* He could push through this. He had to, for Dalton's sake.

Steeling himself, he shuffled forward. Keeping his torso as still as possible, he looked down between his feet. No phone there. Cautiously, he leaned sideways, fighting against the hurt, to check the passenger side. Nothing. *Shit*. It might have been thrown clear of the car, through the broken window. It could be anywhere.

He was no good to Dalton here.

He reached for the door handle and was knocked dizzy by the pain in his right shoulder. Sucking air through gritted teeth, he tried again. It wouldn't open. *No, don't do this*. With a fresh intake of breath, he tried again and managed to release it.

Thank God.

Antoni swung his legs around and was relieved to find they were working okay. He stepped out of the car and straightened. The pain subsided to a throbbing ache once he stood.

The car was in a ditch at the side of the road. The passenger front end had struck a tree and was buckled around the base. He scanned the surrounding area, searching for the light of his phone. Nothing. What were the chances of it still working anyway?

The police had said they would dispatch the next available car to investigate his call. He prayed that wouldn't be long, as it might already be too late. He hadn't known when he'd made the call that Catherine was armed, anyway. They wouldn't send a firearms team to investigate without that knowledge.

She had a gun, and she had Dalton.

The bitch was capable of anything.

She had to be stopped.

Fighting the pain in his chest and shoulder, Antoni climbed the uneven bank out of the ditch.

* * * *

The headlights illuminated the interior of the huge barn. Dalton immediately spotted a decaying work bench in the far corner and an array of rusted instruments. Any one of them would make an efficient weapon. *Too late now.* He was stuck in the car with his maniac sister and whatever plan she was making to get herself out of this mess. She was thinking of places she could take him and kill him, while still making her kidnap story seem plausible. Dalton had no doubt of that fact.

He eased his foot off the clutch, causing the car to stall and buying himself a few more seconds to think. He had to stop worrying about Catherine's plans and think of one of his own. Antoni was in the wreck of that car and most likely injured. Dalton needed a way to get to him.

"Do that again, and I'll shoot you here," Catherine snapped from the back seat.

"Good luck making that fit your version of events. A bullet in the back of my head will hardly sit well with your bullshit kidnap tale."

She jabbed him in the shoulder with the gun. "I'll think of something if it comes to that. Now, start this fucking car and get us out of here."

He stepped on the clutch and pressed the ignition again. The barn was big enough for him to execute a U-turn. His heart sank as he faced forward and the headlights picked up Justin's body, lying in a wide pool of blood.

"Unless you want to join him, I suggest you get moving."

Justin lay in the centre of the courtyard. Dalton eased the car around it to avoid running over him.

"Did you feel anything for him?" he asked.

"Yeah. I felt he could be useful," she crowed. "Turns out I was right. I am about most things."

As he inched around the body at an angle, Dalton noticed the low stone wall that bordered part of the property, around fifty yards ahead of him. He would have to turn right again to straighten the car and get it back onto the road. *Or maybe not.*

This might be the only chance he got.

He paused, pretending to look through the side window at Justin, preparing himself.

"He seemed like a nice guy," he said.

"You would say that." Catherine scoffed. "He was a man. You're all as stupid as each other."

In the rear-view mirror, he saw her attention was also on the corpse. She had fallen for the distraction.

Dalton pressed his foot down hard, flooring the accelerator. The speed gauge shot up to thirty, forty, fifty. He slid the gears into second then third. The engine roared in protest.

In the rear Catherine was unbalanced as the car raced forward, thrown into the corner.

"Noooo," she screamed and fired.

The bullet shot past Dalton's head, smashing through the side window.

He reacted on instinct, ducking, closing his eyes, steeling his body for impact.

The car had almost reached sixty miles per hour when it hit the wall.

Chapter Twenty-Five

Wincing with every step, Antoni staggered from the ditch to the more even ground of the road. He had barely gathered himself when he heard the scream of the engine by the farmhouse and looked up in time to see the car hurtling towards the wall. He realised what was happening a fraction of a second before the collision. A terrible crunching sound of metal against stone filled the night.

The front of the vehicle buckled, crushing backward on itself.

There was a shatter of glass, and a dark shape flew through the windscreen, across the destroyed bonnet and over the wall.

"Dalton," he cried.

He staggered up the dirt road, ignoring the pain that tore through his upper body with each step. He was lightheaded, unable to draw a decent breath. His ribs were broken, that was a certainty, but he would not—

could not — stop. He battled through the agony, focused on one thing…saving Dalton.

Somehow, he made it to the car, and leaning on its side for support, he staggered around to the driver's side.

Dalton was inside, held securely in the seat belt. *Thank God.*

His head lolled forward. *Please let him be alive.*

Antoni tore open the door.

Dalton started, raising his head. Blood trickled from a wound in his hairline. When his eyes focused on Antoni, he saw relief in them.

"Don't try to move just yet," Antoni told him. "Not until we know what injuries you've got."

"You." Dalton winced, as though even talking was a pain. "Are you all right?"

"I am now. Thank God, you're alive."

He scanned Dalton's seated figure, looking for bleeds. Apart from the one on his head, he could see none.

Dalton leaned back in his seat. "Catherine?"

"I don't know. She was thrown from the car. She's over there, somewhere."

"There's a phone," Dalton said, wincing. "It's in my right sock. Can you reach it?"

"Keep still. I'll try." It took a supreme effort. Antoni lowered to his knees and reached into the car with his good arm. He slid his hand around Dalton's calf. "Can you feel that?"

"Yes. I can feel just about everything — my legs, my arms. I don't think I've done much damage."

Antoni raised the leg of his trousers and slid his fingers into his sock until he located the device. "It's fingerprint locked," he said, handing the phone to Dalton.

"Let me get out of this damned car," Dalton said, releasing the seat belt. He winced again. "I think I might have broken a collar bone."

"We'll have a matching pair," Antoni said grimly, getting to his feet to give Dalton room.

Dalton gasped. "Don't make me laugh. Fuck, that hurts."

He eased himself out of the vehicle and leaned against the side, struggling to catch his breath. "Did you call the police?"

Antoni watched him with concern. There were no apparent outward injuries, but anything could be happening internally. "I did, but they didn't see it as a priority."

"I guess it is now." Dalton unlocked the phone and dialled the emergency number, requesting police and an ambulance, explaining that there were three possible casualties and one deceased.

"Deceased?" Antoni asked when he finished the call.

"Justin. Catherine shot him as soon as we arrived."

At another time, the news might have floored him, but Antoni was too numb from his experience and his concern for Dalton to do anything other than accept it. "Was she...going to kill you?"

"That was her plan. That's how she explained it, anyway. She was going to make out that I kidnapped her and held her here. She'd say she killed me when she got the chance to escape."

Antoni's heart swelled with pain and sorrow for Dalton. It could never compare to his relationship with Roger, but Antoni didn't believe Dalton could be unaffected by what Catherine had done. They were siblings…bonded by blood. The depths of her betrayal and hatred were unfathomable.

"She fucked it up," Antoni said bitterly, reaching out with his good hand to take Dalton's.

"She did, but not before killing Justin — and Larissa, by the sound of it."

"I'm sorry, Dalton. This is terrible. I want to hold you so badly right now, but I don't think either of us are in any fit state."

Dalton moved closer to him. "How badly are you hurt? You look like you've come out of this worse than I have."

"Broken ribs, I think. Possible collar bone. It hurts like hell."

Dalton's eyes widened in the dark. "My God, Antoni. C'mon. You need to sit down. This way, lean against the car."

He shook his head. "No. It's really a lot less painful for me to stand. It's better this way. I promise."

"Can you breathe all right?"

"It's painful, but as long as I take shallow breaths, it's manageable."

"You're sure? I can't lose you now, not after all this."

Despite the pain, Dalton's words filled him with joy. They were together. Catherine's actions couldn't alter that fact. Whatever happened now, they would get through it.

"We should check on her," Antoni said at last. "I saw her tossed in that direction."

Dalton glanced into the darkness beyond the stone wall. "I'm tempted to leave her. Let her suffer until the police get here. But that —"

"Would make us just as bad as she is."

Their eyes locked.

Dalton signed. "Exactly. Stay here. I'll go search for her."

"No," Antoni said. "I'm not leaving you. Not again."

"You're a good man. The best I've ever met." Dalton turned on the flashlight function on his phone. He took Antoni's good hand, and they approached the front of the car.

A twelve-foot section of the wall had collapsed under the impact of the crash, and they stepped over the rubble with ease. Antoni caught his breath a couple of times as pain jarred through his torso, but once they reached the even ground of the moor beyond, it became much easier.

"How far was she thrown?" Dalton asked.

"I'm not sure. It happened so fast, but she came through the window with quite a force. She could be some way off."

A few yards farther on, Antoni spotted something dark in the short grass. Dalton shone his light over. It was Catherine's gun.

"Don't pick it up," Dalton warned. "She used it to kill Justin. Her prints are all over it. Leave it as evidence. It will damn her." He swung the small light back and forth in an arc. It illuminated no more than a few meters to either side. They progressed farther.

Antoni's conscience was torn. If Catherine was dead, all their worries would be over...finished. But he wanted her alive to face justice. The worst of all options was for her to vanish—to disappear like the beast who'd stabbed him last year, leaving so much unresolved trauma for the people left behind.

She must be here, he told himself. He'd watched her smash through that window with terrific force. No one could get away from that unscathed.

"There," Dalton exclaimed, stumbling forward.

Antoni followed at his own pace. His breathing was getting worse...more painful. Could a broken rib have punctured his lung? If he didn't get medical attention soon, this time, he might not be so lucky himself.

She lay on her front, her arms spread wide. One look at the unnatural angle of her left leg and he knew it was broken. The right leg didn't look too perfect, either.

"Is she alive?" he asked.

Dalton dropped to his knees beside her, feeling her wrist. The seconds seemed to stretch into hours. "There's a pulse," he said at last.

Antoni gave a silent thanks in relief. If Catherine Caine survived her injuries, she would face a long time in jail, possibly the rest of her life. For the sake of everyone else, prison would be the safest place for her.

"Don't try to move her," he said. "Look at her legs. There could be damage to her spine. You might make it worse."

Dalton turned away from his sister. Antoni caught the pained look that passed over his face and knew the cause was nothing physical. Antoni stepped towards him.

"Are you all right?"

Dalton wiped the back of his hand across his face. Moisture glistened in the torch light. He nodded and rose unsteadily to his feet. They took each other's hand. It was the only comfort their injuries would allow.

"It's cold," Dalton said. "We should cover her until help arrives."

"There's a blanket in the boot of my car."

They retraced their steps together, back to the crumpled wall and onto the farm road. Antoni waited at the top of the bank while Dalton clambered down to retrieve the blanket from the rear. In the quiet of the night, he heard a sound in the distance.

A siren. And flashing blue lights were winding their way towards them.

Dalton climbed back up to join him, and they watched a procession of emergency lights coming across the moor.

Antoni caught something from the corner of his eye. He turned to the east and saw the golden rays of the sun casting a glow on the horizon. "Look," he whispered, and they turned together.

Dawn had arrived.

The long, ugly night was over.

Chapter Twenty-Six

Five months later

It was a day at the end of a remarkably hot summer. The reporters and press photographers who gathered on the steps of Newcastle Crown Court sweltered in the direct glare of the early afternoon sun. Dalton and Antoni had arrived early, ahead of the crowds, and waited in the air-conditioned interior.

"Look at them," Dalton said, jerking his thumb towards the eager press pack. "Catherine has finally achieved the fame and attention she thinks she deserves. They wouldn't have turned out for her before any of this."

Antoni grimaced and fidgeted with the knot of his tie. "I'm glad they're bringing her in the back way, and she won't get to experience it. She doesn't deserve the satisfaction of seeing this. I hope they keep a blanket over her head from the prison van to the dock."

Dalton couldn't argue with Antoni's opinion. He was right. The huge crowd out the front was everything his sister had ever dreamed of. It would be a small justice for her victims to deny her the satisfaction.

The last five months had been a rollercoaster, often seeming like the nightmare ride would never end. Catherine's survival had been touch and go for the first few days, but she had pulled through. The injuries she'd received in the crash meant she would never walk again. She had only been discharged from the hospital into the care of the prison four weeks earlier, allowing the Crown Prosecution Service to proceed with the charges against her.

Today would be the start of a new ordeal. The charges would be presented to her by the court, and she would get the chance to enter her plea. Dalton had no doubt what that would be. She would enter a not guilty plea, meaning a lengthy trial at a future date. Everyone involved in the case would have to give evidence against her. Antoni and he would be called as witnesses. The families of her victims would have to listen as the barbaric details of her crimes were dissected by the lawyers. Some of them were here today.

He recognised Larissa Crawford's brother and sister. Justin Darvill's adult children were also there with his ex-wife.

His own family had made the trip north for the short hearing, too — his mother and father, his brother Tobias. Catherine would undoubtedly think they had come to gloat over her misfortune, but they were there to support Dalton and Antoni as well as offer their condolences to the victims' next of kin. None of them would take any satisfaction from seeing her in the dock.

Just before two o'clock they were ushered into the public gallery of the court. Antoni took his hand, and they walked in together, their heads held high.

"Are you okay?" Antoni whispered as they shuffled to their seats.

"I'm fine," he answered, squeezing his hand in reply.

They had been inseparable since that ill-fated night in March. They had supported each other in their recovery. The broken shoulders and ribs they had both sustained were slow to heal. The mental injuries took longer. Antoni had been through it all before. Dalton had worried that the ordeal might set him back, but Antoni had been strong enough for both of them. Together, they had gotten better.

Things still weren't perfect. A sudden pain could flare up from one of the old breaks, but Dalton had learned to cope with it, while the nightmares continued to haunt his sleep. They might bother him for years, but he knew that he could handle them, because of Antoni.

From their tiered seats, they had a clear view as the door at the rear of the dock opened.

Dalton caught his breath as Catherine was wheeled into the court. There were three security guards present. One pushed the wheelchair while the other two were handcuffed to each of her arms. Antoni tightened his hold on Dalton's hand.

"She can't hurt you anymore. I don't think she'll hurt anyone ever again," Antoni said softly.

Murmurs broke out around the courtroom. The members of the press who had been allowed in were suddenly very active, conversing with each other while scribbling in their notebooks. Catherine's eyes flicked towards them.

I was right. It's the attention she craves, no matter the cost.

The security guards unlocked the handcuffs and stepped towards the rear of the dock.

Catherine's expression was one of thoughtful satisfaction. She looked the same as he'd always remembered. The court staff must have allowed her access to makeup and a black suit for her appearance. Her dark hair was fastened in a ponytail. Her mouth was a red gash. She looked like she was done up for a corporate event or a working lunch. It appeared to Dalton that she was about to snap her next Instagram shot rather than face charges in a crown court.

Her focus moved from the press pack and found him without searching. She caught him in her stare, and a self-satisfied smirk played over her lips.

A chill ran down his spine, and he shuddered.

There's no remorse. No empathy. No regret.

The judge called for the charges to be put to her — the murders of Larissa Crawford and Justin Darvill, and the attempted murders of Dalton Caine and Antoni Nowak.

"How do you plead?" the judge asked.

She paused, milking her moment in the spotlight.

This was her one chance to do the right thing — to plead guilty and spare everyone involved the distress of a trial.

Her mouth widened into a wicked smile, and she said, "Not guilty."

Dalton sighed. He'd been a fool to expect anything else.

* * * *

Antoni surveyed the flat—the place he'd thought of as home for so long. Most of the furniture remained, but all his personal stuff had gone. The previous weekend he'd hired a transit van and transported everything he wanted to Surrey. The flat was going to be rented fully furnished, and the new tenant would collect the keys from Roger in a few days' time.

There was really no reason for him to be here. Everything had already been taken care of, but he wanted one last look around. He had to say goodbye to the place.

He'd asked Dalton to wait downstairs. This was something he had to do alone. He'd expected to feel some kind of regret or sadness, but there was none of that, just a desire to leave it behind and move on with his life...his new life.

It was time.

He walked through the bedroom, stuck his head into the bathroom and the kitchen. There was no sentiment, no painful attachment to the place. This was no longer his home. He had known that for a while.

Dalton was waiting in the alley when he let himself out and locked the door. Leaning against the car, checking out his phone, he straightened at the sight of Antoni and shoved the phone away.

"Everything okay?" he asked, locking eyes.

"It is," Antoni said...and meant it. "There's nothing left up there for me."

Dalton nodded. He knew not to make a scene.

Antoni had asked Roger and the rest of the family to stay away while he left. There was no need for any big drama or drawn-out goodbyes. Antoni was turning his back on Nyemouth, not his family. Besides, he'd be back soon enough. Catherine's trial was scheduled for the end of November. Antoni and Dalton were the main witnesses against her. They would have to return to give evidence. He would always return for Christmas and other special events. He would never be far away from the family he loved. But for now, after everything he'd been through in the last year, he needed to escape this town.

When Dalton had asked Antoni to move in with him, he had never felt happier—a new beginning in a new town with the man he would sacrifice everything for.

Dalton had been refurbishing a large three-bedroom terrace house with a view to selling it once he was finished. "Maybe I don't have to sell it," he'd said the first time Antoni had visited and fallen in love with the house. "It was too big for me alone, but for two of us and maybe a couple of cats, it could be just right."

Antoni slung his bag onto the back seat of Dalton's car and slid a hand around his waist, moving in for a kiss. Dalton put his arms around him and held him until he was ready. Antoni had always believed that home was a place, but now he understood that home could be anywhere. It was the people he shared it with that made it special.

"I love you," he murmured against Dalton's neck.

Dalton hugged him tighter. "I love you, too, darling—more than anything."

After a few moments, he said, "Let's go."

Dalton relaxed his hold. "You're sure?"

Antoni nodded. "This is not my life anymore. My new life is with you."

They got into the car and Dalton pulled slowly down the back street until they reached the main road.

"Want me to stop anywhere before we go?"

Antoni gazed across at him and shook his head.

As they drove over the bridge, he took one last look around the harbour, at the places he used to adore — the bars, cafés and restaurants in the marina, the lifeboat station, even the two ancient piers at the mouth of the river. He wondered if he would ever feel the same about them. Nothing was impossible, but for now, all he wanted was to get out and start his new life in the south with Dalton.

There were too many painful memories here. He wanted to embrace the future — new beginnings, free from violence, and terror, and killing. With Dalton, Antoni felt safe. He was protected and loved. He couldn't say that about Nyemouth.

They would complete the house together — a solid foundation for their future.

As Dalton drove out of the town, Antoni's spirit lifted, like a cloud of oppression had cleared from above him. His heart surged with love for the man beside him and hope for the life that lay before them…a life they would share together.

The possibilities were endless, and no one would ever come between them again.

Want to see more from this author?
Here's a taster for you to enjoy!

Closer by Morning
Thom Collins

Excerpt

Matt Blyth was not a morning man. When his alarm went off at five a.m. it shocked him awake. *What the hell?* Dragged rudely out of dreamland, where he'd been sailing across the Atlantic on a luxury cruise ship, to the darkness of his bedroom on Monday morning. Then he remembered the reason for the alarm. Boot camp. Today would be his first session. What had made him think that was a good idea?

He forced himself out of bed. *No time to think about this. Just do it.*

He stumbled to the bathroom and threw water in his face and raked wet fingers through his dark, wavy hair. Ten minutes later, dressed in joggers and running shoes, he was out of the house. He felt nauseated with the lack of sleep but pushed through it. Minor discomfort would not deter him, not when he was set on doing something he wanted. He was twenty-eight years old. In a little over a year he would turn thirty, that first great milestone of age. He was determined to be in his best shape ever when the dreaded day came. Even if it meant getting up well before dawn to slog it out and sweat for an hour before work.

The morning, which felt like the dead of night, was damp and cold. The sky was still ink black as he steered his car off the estate and onto the road that would take him out of town. It wasn't far to the assembly point, a little over two miles. Soon, when he got used to these God-awful early rises, he wouldn't need the car, he would jog to the meeting place. But not yet. Not today.

Matt turned on the radio. Music usually got him going but the radio was tuned to a local station, just in time for the news. He let it play. He liked to know what was happening in the area, as well as getting the sports results and weather.

The lead item blasted away the final cobwebs of sleep.

"*Durham Police have cordoned off an area of the river bank in the city following the discovery of a body late last night. Police refuse to speculate whether the death is connected to that of student Conner Welsh, whose body was discovered just two weeks ago downriver of the latest finding. Mr. Welsh was severely beaten before being strangled. Durham FM News will bring you further information on the latest death as we receive it.*"

Two bodies dragged from the river within a fortnight. That was unheard of in a small city like Durham. Murder of any kind was rare. He hoped the latest death was nothing more than an accident — a tragic coincidence — in no way connected to the murdered student. Drunk students had always been drawn to the riverbank. Too much alcohol and a loss of balance could have fatal consequences. From what he'd heard, Conner Welsh, the previous victim, suffered a nightmare ordeal before going in the water. He prayed it hadn't happened again.

The story continued to trouble him as he followed the winding country road, though he tuned out the rest of the bulletin and missed the sports update. The image of the murdered student had been a regular feature in the local press these last two weeks. A smiling, happy boy. Young and good-looking, a university student, Conner had everything to smile about. But some sick bastard had thought otherwise. Matt hoped they quickly found who was responsible, for the sake of Conner's family and the wider community.

Thin fingers of light began to crawl across the sky when he pulled into the car park at Binchester Woods. A handful of vehicles were already parked and a group of people in sports clothes were limbering up and stretching against the picnic table.

So there were others just as crazy as he was, coming out to exercise at this early hour.

There was no sign of Annabel's Fiat among the parked cars. Typical. This crazy venture was her idea. "C'mon, Matt," she had enthused in the office kitchen. "We'll motivate each other. And think how great it will be to get it over with so early in the day. No more having to drag our tired butts to the gym after work. Our evenings will be our own."

He had texted her the night before to make sure she was still up for the challenge.

Definitely she had replied and had added a smiley face.

Matt locked the car and headed toward the group of people. There were four men and three women, all of them swaddled in layers from head to foot.

"Is this the meeting point for boot camp?" he asked, certain it must be. Why would they be here otherwise?

A large man stepped forward. He carried a hardback notebook and a pencil. "It is. I'm Clint. I'm instructing the group today."

"Hi." They shook hands. "You spoke to my work colleague on the phone. Annabel Faith. She made the booking for both of us."

Clint consulted his little notebook. "Matt, is it?" He ticked him off his list. "Is your friend with you?"

"No. But she only has to come from town. She shouldn't be long." She had better not be.

Clint was huge. Exactly how Matt imagined a boot camp instructor would look—an enormous, ex-military, brick shithouse. With his steely crew cut and dark, hooded eyes, he looked like a hard case who would take no prisoners. He was sexy too, in a strange, scary way. Not really Matt's type, but he could see the appeal.

Clint enquired about his current level of fitness.

"Decent, I'd say. I train at the gym three or four times a week and like to run at weekends. I eat plenty of protein and take it easy with carbs. I'm just looking to improve my overall levels of fitness." All true, if slightly exaggerated.

Clint looked him over closely before making notes in his book. "Good. Any health concerns I should know about before you start?"

"None."

"Sure? This is an intense course."

"That's what I'm looking for. Something I can't get at the gym."

Clint nodded, satisfied, and closed his book. "You've come to the right group. Whipping bodies into shape, that's what I'm known for. No messing, no time wasting, no excuses—just exceptional results. A guy in my group last year made the front cover of *Men's Health* magazine. Those are the kind of results I aim for."

Matt stretched while they waited for the rest of the group to arrive. Clint told him they would leave at five-forty-five sharp. "Get here later than that and we'll be gone."

There was still no sign of Annabel. Punctuality wasn't one of her strong points. If she intended to turn up at all. Knowing her, she would still be curled beneath her duvet. He was mad for listening to her in the first place. She never came through, always full of enthusiastic ideas but with little success in achieving them.

More vehicles began to pile into the car park and soon there was a group of around twenty assembling for the class. They were mainly men, aged twenty through to mid-forties. Intense, serious-looking men who didn't mess about over fitness. Real go-hard-or-go-home types. Maybe it was a factor of the unsociable hour, but there wasn't much conversation going on. That suited Matt. Nobody wanted small talk at this time of day.

He cast an appraising eye over the group. They were fit, masculine, real men's men, but, a little bit like Clint, he found them rather asexual. Not his type at all. Not that he was looking anyway, but hey, a little eye candy could provide great motivation.

Just before the appointed start time another vehicle pulled into the car park and a man in blue running pants and a gray hoodie jumped out and jogged toward Clint. They spoke briefly and the instructor made a few hurried notes in his book.

Matt's interest was piqued by the new arrival. This was more like it. Even from a distance, he could see this guy was something very special. With short, dark blond hair and a light beard, he was as manly as the rest of the group but seemed to lack the focused intensity that made them so fearsome.

He even smiled as he left Clint to join the group. A lovely, winning smile that wrinkled the corners of his sparkly eyes and illuminated a broad, handsome face.

"Hi, guys," he addressed the group as a whole in a warm American accent.

"Hi," Matt replied while the others responded with a non-committal grunt or nod.

Unselfconsciously, the newcomer began to stretch.

Matt found it hard not to stare. Wow. This guy looked good from a distance but was even better close up. He had the broad build of a man in his thirties and, though he was swaddled in layers like the rest of them, Matt could discern the strong lines of his shoulders and butt through that clothing.

But it was his face, with its twinkly eyes and golden skin, that was so exceptionally handsome.

Matt, with his wavy brown hair, brown eyes and angular face, was good-looking. He wasn't vain or conceited about it, he knew he was attractive, but couldn't help feeling inadequate beside the glorious American. With a face like that, he could do anything he wanted and the world would accept it — model, actor, politician, king.

Take it easy. Matt turned away. It was the only way to keep from staring.

He had the beginnings of an erection.

He'd wanted eye candy and now he had it. He'd have to be careful that the American didn't become a distraction rather than a motivation.

Clint Dexter's boot camp was advertised as the toughest, most effective workout in the county. *Hard work and effort get results!* proclaimed the poster in the window of his town center fitness studio. *Nobody trains you harder.*

It was no lie.

Without equipment, weights or gimmicks, Clint pushed his group on the most intense and physically grueling workout Matt had ever known. Clint was old school in his methods. Like an army sergeant breaking in the new recruits, he drove them uphill and into the woods. There was no let-up. He shouted and blew whistles, breaking up the run with demands for press-ups, squats, lunges, then straight back onto the track, going higher up the steep hill. There were no breaks. No moment to catch a breath.

Matt believed he was in good shape. Epic mistake. Every muscle in his body seemed to ache. His lungs were ablaze as he drew one arduous breath after another. *Shit.* He'd never known anything like this. And it didn't stop. For the whole hour Clint worked them hard—no slacking, no respite.

Matt was glad to see he wasn't the only one struggling with the course. He might be the newbie but even the seasoned old-timers were taking it badly. Everyone was red-faced and grimacing with pain.

Finally Clint guided them back down to the car park. It was over.

"Make sure you all stretch down thoroughly," he shouted as he walked among the group. Most people were bent double, clutching their knees and gasping. "You'll pay for it later if you don't take the time now."

"Some group, eh?"

Matt realized that he was standing beside the handsome American. The course was so exhausting that he'd stopped paying attention to the blond hunk after the first five minutes. His hair was soaked, plastered to his head, and his face burned red, yet he exuded a sexiness that would have caught Matt's breath if he wasn't already wrecked.

Matt struggled to speak. "My first time," he gasped.

"Yeah? Me too. I thought I was fit until this morning. This guy has destroyed me."

"I doubt anyone is fit enough for this."

The American laughed. "You could be right. I've had personal trainers in the past. Let me tell you, none of them worked me half as hard as this dude. Not ever."

"Think you'll do it again?"

"Absolutely. A month of this and we could compete as Iron Men."

"You might be right. If we survive a month. My heart might not be able to take it."

"I'm Dale," he said. "Hi."

"Hello. I'm Matt."

"Nice to meet you, Matt," Dale said cheerily.

Matt was struck again by just *how* good-looking Dale was. God, his eyes—they were as blue as a cloudless August sky.

As he stretched his tired muscles, Matt tried not to be affected by the proximity of Dale, but it wasn't easy. It wasn't just the way he looked, it was his manner and the confidence he exuded. Even the smell of him, the sweat from all that hard work, was an aphrodisiac. It was a long time, if ever, since a man had had such a devastating effect on him. When Dale bent over to touch his toes and gave Matt the full benefit of his glorious rump, he had to turn away. Tenting the front of his pants with a hard-on was *not* the kind of first-day impression he wanted to make.

The sun finally put in an appearance, breaking weakly through the clouds above the jagged tree line.

"I've got to beat it," Dale said, straightening up and thrusting a hand at Matt. "Will you be here for the next session?"

Matt took his hand and was transfixed by those eyes. This must be how a rabbit feels as he's about to become road kill. "Wednesday? Yes, I'll be here." Truthfully, he hadn't been sure he had more than one early start a week in him, but that was before he met Dale. If he needed a reason to drag his tired butt out of bed, this was as good as he'd find.

"Great. I'm glad to see I'm not the only new guy. We're in this together now. Got to give those regular guys a run for their money, don't you think? So I'll see you Wednesday. Bye for now, Matt."

Dale jogged toward his car, giving Matt one final glimpse of his beautiful bouncing butt.

What was that? Matt felt as though he'd been picked up, spun around and dropped back down again. Had Dale been flirting? Or was that just American friendliness? Probably, Matt reasoned. He was so used to British reserve and surliness that he'd misread the signs. Dale was being friendly, that was all.

He shouldn't hope for more.

About the Author

Thom Collins is the author of Closer by Morning, with Pride Publishing. His love of page turning thrillers began at an early age when his mother caught him reading the latest Jackie Collins book and promptly confiscated it, sparking a life-long love of raunchy novels.

Thom has lived in the North East of England his whole life. He grew up in Northumberland and now lives in County Durham with his husband and two cats. He loves all kinds of genre fiction, especially bonkbusters, thrillers, romance and horror. He is also a cookery book addict with far too many titles cluttering his shelves. When not writing he can be found in the kitchen trying out new recipes. He's a keen traveler but with a fear of flying that gets worse with age, but since taking his first cruise in 2013 he realized that sailing is the way to go.

Thom loves to hear from readers. You can find his contact information, website details and author profile page at https://www.firstforromance.com/

PUBLISHING

Sign up for our newsletter and find out about all our romance book releases, eBook sales and promotions, sneak peeks and FREE romance books!